Whispers from the Bay

Whispers from the Bay

A Dolphin Chronicles Book

John S. Tkac

Southeast Books

Published by Southeast Books, Inc.

Library of Congress Control Number: 2007902049
ISBN-10: 0-9794454-0-X
ISBN-13: 978-0-9794454-0-8

Cover design by First Team Advertising

www.whispersfromthebay.com
www.southeastbooks.com

Printed in Canada

To my family and friends
for their love and understanding

Author's Note

This portrayal of dolphin life is based on scientific fact as well as fiction. The descriptions of Key Biscayne, Miami, the Bahamas, and the surrounding waters contain elements of historical, geographical, and scientific accuracy, but in the final analysis, are mythical in nature. Any resemblance to actual events or persons living or dead is purely coincidental.

Contents

Prologue

Two dolphins barely broke the surface and arched forward. Their dorsal fins sliced through the tranquil waters and then disappeared below as the sun hammered down on the bay. They hurried toward Miami, moving at a steady pace, past the steel-gray lighthouse and the island.

Come on. Let's keep moving, Leda urged her mate.

I'm right with you, Padin thought. *Are you sure you know where we're going?*

Yes. The others followed the boat that brought him. They're over there on the coast at Saint Mary's. Leda let out a screech of sound in the water, as an ordinary dolphin might. A whistle came back. She and Padin swam toward the sound, joining four other dolphins circling in the bay.

Has anybody heard from him? Leda asked.

No, none of us have heard or felt anything since they put him on the boat to bring him here, a mind offered. *We think he must be dead.*

Leda turned to the others. *There's no need for all of us to stay here. I'll try to make contact with him.*

We are all friends of Archie's, Leda, we should all stay.

If Archie survived the attack, his mind is probably very weak, Leda sent. *It would be better if only one of us tried to contact him.*

The dolphins agreed and moved out of the bay and then to the east, while Leda swam toward the hospital.

Archie, are you there? Can you hear me? Archie, can you speak to me?

Archibald Pickens had died, as the dolphins would learn officially the next day from the Teachers at the great dome. Leda knew it instinctively, but continued to reach out to him through her loss.

Come on, Archie, speak to me. Archie, can you feel my mind?

Leda reluctantly gave up. She dove to the bottom and then turned, pointed her nose upward, and burst through the surface, flying high in the air. Her mind shouted out, *Good-bye, Archie! We'll always love you!*

Archie couldn't feel her mind, but someone else in the hospital could.

Chapter 1
Mike and the Key

Gazing from the hospital window at the bay and her island home beyond, Alice Connelly held her new baby boy. Her husband, Jim, would be along soon to take them home. The baby squirmed and whimpered. "There, there, Michael."

Michael Connelly cried as Alice turned to the window. Out in the bay a dolphin reached the apex of a magnificent leap. It spun in the air, curved back over, and splashed into the water. Alice rocked her baby boy. "Don't cry, Michael, everything is just fine."

A nurse bustled through the half-opened door. "Hello, Mrs. Connelly. Ready to go?"

"Oh, yes. I'm waiting for my husband. I just saw a beautiful dolphin jump out in the bay."

"We see them all the time. They come around quite a bit when we're wheeling patients out by the water to get some air. You know, this is one of the hospitals assigned to care for our soldiers who have been wounded in the fighting in Europe."

Alice shook her head. "I've seen them. It's horrible." She sighed.

The nurse nodded. "Some of the soldiers who have sufficiently recovered go to our beach, float around, and get some sun. On many days, the dolphins come and gently play and swim with the men. Some of the nurses believe that the dolphins understand and are trying to help the sick, but I don't know. One of our doctors actually prescribes swimming with the dolphins to men who are having trouble adjusting."

"I can't believe it. How interesting!"

"To me it's just strange. The doctor claims it works, and that he has watched men with severe battle fatigue improve after a few sessions with the dolphins."

The women smiled at each other.

"Here is Mike's birth certificate. Keep it in a safe place." The nurse handed Alice the document. Alice smiled as she read the words:

Michael Garrison Connelly

Born: July 25, 1944.

"Good luck, Mrs. Connelly." The nurse turned and walked out of the room.

The black 1937 Chevy sedan turned out of the hospital parking lot onto the tree-lined street. The huge branches of the banyan trees spread across the street from both sides. They grew together high above the road, sending thin little strands of brown, hair-like roots reaching for the ground. When the roots grew long enough to touch the earth, they dug in and formed thick trunks to support more overarching limbs of the great trees.

"I've always liked these big banyans," Alice said. "They keep the streets nice and cool. It's like driving through a green tunnel."

Jim smiled at her. Even under the trees, the sun peeked through. Their new little baby boy slept in her arms, despite the hot, steamy weather. The heat and humidity caused Mike's light brown baby hair to stick against his head. Alice fanned him.

Jim watched the road ahead. "He sure is a good baby—not a whimper. How are you feeling?"

"Fine, I'm just a little tired."

The car glided onto a causeway surrounded by pale green and blue water stretching south toward the rest of the Keys. Alice gazed out over the mottled bay. The water changed from green to blue to purple as clouds drifted over and cast their shadows on the surface.

She nuzzled her baby boy and thought, *That dolphin jumping near the seawall at the hospital, that was a good sign, Michael.*

The island of Key Biscayne lay off the coast, east and a little south of Miami, in the warm, clear ocean. The sedan continued across the bridges and onto the key, where more banyan trees hung over the road. Behind the trees, the mangrove swamp grew dense and dark.

As they rounded the turn, they popped out from beneath the spreading trees and into the sunlight. Hibiscus bushes dotted with thousands of pink, red, and yellow blossoms grew on the median down the middle of the street. White tile roofs glistened in the sun. The colors of the stucco houses—pastel pinks, yellows, and greens—paled in comparison with the colors of the flowers.

Jim slowed the car as they neared the only shopping center on the Key. Twelve stores stood in a long, low strip between the A&P grocery and Connelly's Drugs & Sundries.

"Would you mind if we stopped at the store, just for five minutes? I want to show Mike to everyone."

Alice shook her head and they pulled into the parking lot. Palms grew from little grassy patches in the asphalt. Jim jumped out, ran around and opened the passenger door. As Alice swung her feet out, Jim reached down and helped her out of the car and then took the baby.

Inside the store, eighteen chrome stools with bright red seats stood in front of the lunch counter, bolted to the black-and-white checked tile floor. The lunch counter served as an informal gathering place for many of the Key's residents. Rows of shelves held knick-knacks, souvenirs, and beach towels, and a rack of suntan oils stood near the front door. A card table held bottles of a local concoction, which consisted of Johnson's Baby Oil and iodine—a little sign on the table guaranteed visitors a golden brown Florida tan. The smell of *coco butter* filled that part of the store. The dark brown wooden blades of twelve ceiling fans slowly stirred the air.

Jim boomed out, "Ladies and gentlemen, may I present the newest member of the Connelly clan, Michael Garrison Connelly!"

Wearing a white apron that accented her teak-colored skin, Rosa Hernandez stood behind the counter, her brown hair pulled behind her head. "Come here, Mr. C. Let me hold little Miguel," Rosa said. Jim handed the bundle to Rosa. "Oh how beautiful," Rosa sang out.

"Where are the boys?" Rosa walked around the end of the counter, and gave Mike back to Alice.

"At my mom's in town."

Rosa nodded, "Would you like some coffee, Alice?"

"No thanks, how about some lemonade?"

"How about you, Mr. C?"

"No thanks, Rosa, nothing for me."

Joan Riley, the store's other employee, came around the shelves. "Congratulations, Alice," she said, peeking at Mike. "Any problems?"

"He's just fine, but I'm a little tired."

"Sure you are, dear. Jim, why don't you get Alice home? We'll have plenty of time to be around this boy, and, I've got six prescriptions here that need to be filled." She pointed to the papers on the counter. "One is for Mrs. Medina." Joan tilted her head over her left shoulder.

A slender Spanish woman, her back ramrod-straight, her pale olive skin weathered, walked around the end of the aisle toward Jim. She held a big straw hat in one hand, and her starched white dress fell to her ankles.

"Hello, Jim. Congratulations." She gave Jim a slight hug.

"Thank you, Carmen. I'll have your prescription in a while."

"Oh, no hurry; I sometimes think a glass of fresh coco milk and a cup of strong coffee are better than any medicine you have here."

"You might be right, Carmen."

"So where is the baby?" The old woman walked past Jim toward Alice. When she stood in front of Alice, her eyes crinkled and she touched her forehead.

"Are you all right?"

Carmen smiled. "Oh yes," but she quickly sat on one of the stools at the counter.

"May I?" She reached out.

"Of course." Alice handed the baby to Carmen.

The old woman bent over the baby in her lap. Her eyes crinkled up again.

"Are you sure you're okay?" Alice asked, as she noticed Carmen's wince.

"I'm fine, just a little buzzing in my head. Another beautiful boy and, I believe, a very special boy." She kissed the baby's forehead.

Alice took the baby back. "Thank you, Carmen."

As Jim closed the car door, Alice glanced toward the store. Carmen stood at the plate glass window staring out at the car. They pulled away from the store and Alice noticed Carmen continuing her intense stare.

"Here you are, Mike." Alice smiled a contented, comfortable smile. "Home sweet home."

The pale green house had white shutters, a white garage door, and a white tile roof, much the same as most of the other simple houses being built around the Key. Behind the house, an inlet led into the blue-green bay. Across the inlet's fifty feet of azure water lay the coconut plantation owned by the Medina family.

Jim carried a suitcase into the house, and Alice carried Mike.

Flip-flap, flip-flap—the doggie door at the end of the glassed-in back porch signaled the arrival of Rocky, a big, tan Lab with floppy ears, who bounced over to Jim. He wagged his tail so hard, his entire body swung back and forth. Jim smiled, "Hey, boy, I just want to be half the man you think I am."

Alice bent down. "Come here, boy. Here's another little Connelly to watch over. Rocky, this is Mike."

Rocky sniffed and stared at the bundle and then padded over to Jim for a scratch.

"I'm going to put the baby down to nap for a while."

"I have to go back to the store." Jim headed for the door.

"Be home early. Remember, my mom is bringing the boys back and she's bringing dinner."

Jim waved over his shoulder.

Alice put Mike down in the crib, as the fan spun silently above him. The little baby lay on the crisp, cool sheet with nothing covering him.

She sat in the sun-filled glass room and stared out at the backyard, the dock, the strip of water, and the thick grove of coconut palms on the Medina's side. She thought about her gorgeous new baby with his dark brown eyes and light brown hair that she knew would turn blond in the intense tropical sun.

A comforting, and almost perfect, world surrounded Alice. She and Jim had moved from Miami to the island after Jim had returned from the War. Being wounded in North Africa had made him a bit of a celebrity on the Key, and the drug store flourished. The causeway from the mainland, finished four years ago, had brought many more families to the sun-drenched island.

The next summer, a group of dolphins swam close to Key Biscayne on the bay side. Dolphin families living around Key Biscayne found the people there to be kind and gentle. From time to time they frolicked near humans just for the sport of it. For the special dolphins, human contact had been a part of their mission in life for a long time.

Let's go up this inlet, Leda said.

Where does it lead, Mom? asked Nyla.

Nowhere, it just ends up here. I think it's a special place.

A much bigger male dolphin, speed-swimming on the surface, came up behind the two females. *Where are you girls going?* Padin asked.

Up here to look at the houses and docks, Leda replied.

Do you still feel something?

Yes, and I'm sure it's not the woman in the house at the end of the island, Leda said.

What do you feel, Mom?

Another special human mind; it is weak, but there is definitely something.

I don't feel anything, Nyla said.

Neither do I, but your mom has always been a bit more sensitive than most of us.

The three dolphins glided by the houses and the wooden docks bolted against the concrete seawall.

It takes time to sense a rare human mind like the one I am feeling now, Leda said.

Do you think the old woman will ever communicate with us? Padin asked.

No, I am sure she feels things, but I don't think she will ever be like Archie.

Do the Teachers know about your feelings? Nyla asked.

Yes, but I've told them there isn't much here for now. Where are the others?

They're out south of the flats in the bay. They'll be balling up some mackerel soon, Padin said.

The dolphins turned around and picked up their pace as they swam back toward the bay. Leda spun back at the mouth of the inlet.

Now what? Padin asked.

Leda circled again. *I sense a very young and very special mind.*

Chapter 2

The Dolphins

The dolphins moved around the point. Curving out of the water and then down again, they swam slowly in the channel between the island and the stilt houses. The hue of their thick bodies resembled the color of the light gray clouds in the morning sky. Each dorsal fin, sticking straight up out of a dolphin's back, became a little darker over time, but on their bellies, their skin ranged from a lighter gray to a pinkish white. Some dolphins in this part of the sea wore stripes of varying shades of gray and white down their sides, while other dolphins developed dark and light freckly spots as they grew older. The dolphins' large, round foreheads enabled them to broadcast rapid clicking sounds reminiscent of a rusty hinge creaking as an old door opened. When these clicking sounds bounced off objects and returned, the dolphins sensed the sound waves and used them to visualize objects.

Nyla and Naar, powerful young adult dolphins, left the point of the island behind for the calmer inland waters.

Come on, Naar. Let's go up this inlet, Nyla said.

We might get trapped up there. That inlet is too narrow and shallow and there is only one way out.

Don't worry, she said, *I've been up there with my mother, and people are always around.*

Turning to the right, Nyla started up the inlet. Naar followed next to her and a little behind as his nervousness continued to build. The big male dolphin thought emphatically to his partner. *The inlet ends up here.*

I know. It's okay.

Nyla lifted her head out of the water and saw a yellowish-brown dog lying in the sun on a wooden dock. One paw hung over the edge of the wood, his head rested on the other paw. Next to him, a baby napped in a canvas chair that hung from a metal frame. His fat little legs stuck out of the holes in the bottom. Working quickly, and holding wooden clothespins in her mouth, Nyla watched a woman hang laundry on a line in the yard while attempting to corral two young toddlers playing with a basket of clothes at her feet.

As Nyla's head came out of the water, the hole on the top of her head popped open. *Pfff!* Hot air and spray shot out. The dog perked up and gave an almost silent *gruff.*

Naar—a little baby. Nyla rolled over to one side. Her sparkling black eye stared at the baby. The dog started to bark.

Turn around. That dog could jump on you, Naar sent.

The brown dog whined a little, and then barked louder. Nyla watched the baby for a moment and then slowly began to turn around.

Now noisily flapping his arms and legs, the baby's swing chair began to jiggle.

The woman walked over to the dock and discovered the dolphins below her. "Mike, look at the beautiful dolphins. Quiet, Rocky," she patted the dog's head. Rocky kept barking.

We shouldn't go into places like this. It could be dangerous.

I think the people are interesting, and anyway, Krondal likes to hear about our observations.

Krondal doesn't need us for that.

All right, Naar, all right.

The two dolphins slowly started out of the inlet.

The woman turned to the boys who still tumbled around with the clothes basket. "Will, Bob, hurry—come here boys—dolphins!" The boys waddled down to the dock and their mother quickly grabbed both of them.

Nyla turned back and swam by the dock again—close enough for the boys to almost touch her sleek, shiny body. As she got close—*Pfff*—she spouted hot air again. The boys jumped back squealing with delight, as they felt the spray. Nyla turned, flipped her tail and sprinkled the dock. The boys laughed and their mom laughed louder. Rocky barked crazily while the baby squirmed in his chair, clapping his little hands.

His mom walked over to the baby and patted his head and face dry with the hem of her dress. "The dolphin splashed you, Mike. Was that fun?"

Come on, Nyla, Naar sent. Rocky whined almost imperceptibly. Mike gurgled and wildly flapped his arms and legs.

And, just then, Nyla sensed something—her black eye came out of the water as she again rolled to one side. Nyla focused on the little baby. She wondered whether her feeling matched the sensation her mom had experienced when they swam up this same inlet in the past. She thought to herself that she would visit here often.

Nyla and Naar caught up to the rest of the pod swimming lazily out in the bay. In their normal configuration, the two big males, Eshu and Malak, swam out in front of and to the flanks of the group. Corran and Loa, the other couple, followed the two males with young Farin and Risa behind them.

I think I sensed a human mind up the inlet just now, Nyla announced to the group.

A mind like Archie's? Corran asked.

No, but I did feel something.

Did you feel it, Naar? asked Loa.

No, but I wasn't concentrating.

Let's go out to sea and ball up a school of mackerel or yellow tail and then go to the islands. Nyla changed the subject, but Malak knew what she wanted to do.

Do you want to go to the dome? he asked.

Yes. I want to tell Krondal.

You don't have anything to tell him. You just felt something, Naar said.

Krondal said he didn't want to wait too long for another human contact. This could be important, said Loa.

Let's get something to eat, Naar said.

Three males now fanned out in front of the other five dolphins. They knew a meal would soon come into view as they filled the water with clicks. Picking up the pace, the pod moved into the Gulf Stream and then toward the islands of the Bahamas.

A crystal dome, the size of a big top circus tent, stood on the white sand seabed and rose up to just below the surface. The huge glass bubble sparkled as the sunlight beamed down through the rippling blue-green water.

I'm positive it is a mind we can contact, Nyla said.

Have you identified this human?

No, but I know this new mind is on Key Biscayne.

What of the woman we've spoken about?

Yes, she lives on Key Biscayne as well, and I sense that she can feel us, but she can't break through. Her mind is not powerful enough.

The time will be here soon; we will need another contact by then.

I understand. We'll keep searching.

Chapter 3

School Days

Dr. Samuelson came into the outer office. He wore a white coat over his white shirt and dark tie. Dr. Samuelson smiled. "Hello, Mrs. Connelly, let's go back to my office, Mike is playing with one of the nurses in an examining room."

Alice sat down. "I'm so worried about Mike. Ever since he began talking he has struggled: m-m-mama, d-d-dad, W-W-Will. His brothers are talkative boys and my fear is that Mike is withdrawing. Instead of fighting it, I sense that he has decided to just stay quiet and alone."

"This is normal for someone with a pronounced stutter. Mike has no physical problems and he is a very bright lad."

"How do I keep him from wanting to be alone?" Alice looked down and shook her head.

"For now, just keep talking to him and push him a little to speak to you. Sit down with him and encourage him to read out loud to you. Mrs. Connelly, Mike will be fine. Don't worry—and for heaven's sake, don't let him think that you're worried."

Alice and the doctor stood up. "Thanks for everything."

She found Mike sitting in one of the examination rooms next to a nurse as she read to him.

Alice put her hand on Mike's shoulder and smiled. "Come on big guy, let's head for the Key."

The doctor stood at the door. "Remember Mrs. Connelly, your positive attitude will be important as time goes on." He smiled and gave Alice a reassuring little wink.

"Thank you, Doctor, I understand." Although concerned for her little boy, Alice took hope in the doctor's advice.

Even though he wasn't quite sure how he would get along talking to the kids in his class, Mike couldn't wait to start first grade. The kids in his neighborhood teased him about his stuttering, but in time they got over it, and so had he. Mike knew that some of the kids at school would laugh and snicker at him, and he was prepared for that—at least that's what he told himself. Will and Bob, in the second and third grades, informed Mike that they'd show him around. The two older boys had already placed their plaid canvas book bags in the wire baskets on their Schwinn bikes.

"Come on, Mike," Will called to him, "we'll show you where to go."

Alice smiled at her three boys—dressed in their new navy slacks and sneakers. "Boys, I'm going with you this morning."

"Mom, you don't have to," the two older boys whined in unison.

"No, boys, I'm coming, so ride next to me. I'll walk. This is Mike's first day."

Will and Bob circled in the street. Mike frowned up at mom a little.

Alice smiled at him and rubbed his sandy-blond hair. "I know, Mike. I want to say hello to your teacher."

The planners of Key Biscayne had built the school in the center of the village. Two long, low, pink buildings, with many jalousie glass windows, faced each other across a well trimmed green courtyard divided by sidewalks and benches. Covered walkways connected rows of classrooms. Offices, the library, and the auditorium filled one end of the courtyard, with an open breezeway for the lunch area at the other end. There, rows of wooden picnic tables sat on the shiny, dark green painted floor, and ceiling fans twirled.

Beyond the lunch area, a great, tree-lined playground awaited the hordes of children. Inside the playground's fence, metal bicycle racks stood in a perfect row. Most of the kids on the Key rode their bikes to school.

Martha Pomerance had been the principal since the school opened ten years before. Earlier that summer, Martha had introduced Jim and Alice to Jane Woodward, the new first-grade teacher. Martha insisted that they could teach Mike; he would not need to go to a "special" school.

Alice found the first-grade room where Jane stood in the doorway, greeting each new arrival. The rows of wooden desks soon filled with talking children. Bookcases stood below the slatted glass windows, and metal fans whirred in the corners of the room.

When Alice walked to the door with Mike, carrying his book bag and lunch box, Jane greeted them. "Hello, Mrs. Connelly."

"Hello, Miss Woodward, this is Mike."

Jane knelt down, making eye contact with Mike. "Hi, Mike. How are you today?"

"O-k-kay."

"Good," Jane smiled. Jane took Mike by the shoulder, and led him to the first desk in the row on the far side of the room. "You sit here, Mike."

Mike sat down. Jane walked back over to Alice. "Don't worry, Mrs. Connelly. Mike will be fine."

With tears in her eyes Alice turned away, grateful that Mike would get a lot of special attention from her friends at this wonderful school.

A girl with curly brown hair sat down next to Mike. "Hi. I'm Molly."

Mike stared at her, and then he took a deep breath, "Hi." He thought the interaction had gone well, but he knew the feeling wouldn't last.

Mike kept quiet for the rest of the morning. He hoped he would not have to speak anytime soon.

At lunchtime, Mike saw his brothers and a neighbor, Rusty, sitting at a long table. "Hi, Mike," Will said. "How's your teacher?"

"O-k-kay, I g-guess."

Lucy Medina sat next to Mike. The same age as Bob, she lived down the street, and had been around Mike and his stuttering for years. "Hi, Mike. How's school?" Lucy asked.

"It's g-good."

Another boy sat down. "Who are you?" he asked Mike.

"I'm M-M-Mike C-C-Connelly."

"C'mon buddy," the boy laughed. "Spit it out."

Lucy glared at him. "Hey, shut up."

"What's the matter, cat got his tongue?" The boy spat back.

Rusty spun in his seat. "He stutters a little. You got a problem with that?"

The boy turned to face Rusty's menacing glare and glanced down at the fist resting on the lunch table. A long moment of silence passed.

"No, I don't have a problem."

"Good, then like she said, shut up about it." Rusty turned back to his sandwich.

Mike glanced at Lucy and then opened his Lone Ranger lunch box.

After school Mike saw his mom standing at the back gate of the schoolyard as he ran with Will and Bob.

"Hi, boys, how did school go today?" she asked.

"Great, Mom," Will said, "Miss McDonald is great."

"We already have homework," Bob said.

Alice turned to Mike and asked, "How did you do with Miss Woodward?"

"Sh-she was f-fine, M-Mom."

Alice came close to Mike as he got on his bike. She touched his shoulder. "Everything go okay?"

"Y-yeah, Mom." Mike pedaled off to catch his brothers and Rusty.

Mike got all A's in the first grade, but when he read out loud, he stuttered. Some of the kids snickered and giggled, and then Mike stuttered even more. Miss Woodward sometimes sat in the corner with Mike and let him read just to her. She would tell him to slow down. Mike liked that, and her coaching helped. But when Mike spoke to anyone, he stuttered. On the playground some kids made fun of him, but Mike never paid too much attention. Bob, Will, and Rusty made it their mission to stick up for Mike, and a few fights came of it, but Mike knew that the fights and protests made no difference. He still stuttered and the kids still snickered at him. Mike learned to keep his feelings inside. Silence became comfortable for Mike—not that he wanted it that way, it's just the way it had to be.

Chapter 4

An Encounter

Whenever the opportunity arose, Jim took the boys fishing, snorkeling, and riding around the bay in the family's little aluminum boat. One early morning, Jim and his boys drifted out in the bay just a little south of the stilt houses which sprouted out of the shallow sandbar. Will had just caught a nice yellowtail, and Bob's pole bent with another one on the line.

Jim encouraged Bob. "Keep reeling, pull him in."

Mike bent over the side. "H-he's r-right under the b-boat. H-he's a b-big one."

As Jim reached for the net, Bob pulled the fish up to the side. The yellowtail bounced around on the bottom of the boat.

"Mike, how many do we have in the ice chest?"

Mike went to the front and opened the lid. "S-seven."

"Okay, boys, let's go swimming over on the flats. Will, drive us over to Mr. Higgins' house. We'll tie up there," Jim said.

Bob squawked, "Hey Dad, it's my turn."

"You can drive us home."

Will pulled on the cord at the top of the little outboard and nothing happened. He pulled again and the motor came to life. Will twisted the throttle arm, and the boat moved forward.

Half a mile off the southern tip of the Key a long sandbar, a few feet below the surface at low tide, stretched back into the bay. Warning ships away from the treacherous water, the new modern lighthouse stood on the ocean side of the shallows. On the sandbar a curious collection of structures rose out of the water; oddly shaped cottages made of wood stood on telephone poles or concrete pilings. The owners of these unusual houses had built them far enough apart for privacy, but close enough together to be recognized as a community. Most of South Florida knew of 'Stiltsville'.

No two structures were shaped alike; some had flat roofs, others slanted. One was shaped like a big capital 'A' with the support pilings touching at the top and the floor of the living area forming the bar across the 'A'. With the South Florida sun beating down and the constant onslaught of the Atlantic wind and waves, the houses of Stiltsville had weathered to a pale, brownish color. The seabirds, of course, saw to it that the buildings sported plenty of white dots and splatters. The docks and stairs up to the porches lay next to or underneath the houses.

On weekends, people brought their families and friends out to fish, to swim, or just to watch the perfect sunsets over the bay, while gulls and pelicans soared overhead. Being a friendly bunch, the people of Stiltsville visited each other's porches, which extended over the aqua blue water. To the delight of the inhabitants, dolphins regularly frolicked below the houses, and barracudas, tarpons, rays, turtles, and the occasional dark shadows of sharks frequented the shallows. Daylight and low tide brought visitors who walked the sandbar, picking up glistening white seashells colored in the subtlest shades of pink, beige, and gray. By afternoon, most of the tourists realized they had been scorched to the color of boiled lobster and would leave the magical beauty of these waters to the locals.

Tying the little boat to the dock next to the stilt house, Jim climbed up on the dock. "Last one in is a rotten egg!" he yelled as they jumped in the water. With the tide at the high mark, the water came up to Jim's chest. The three boys bobbed around in the water and clung to their dad. Mike swam to the ladder on the dock while Will and Bob found a place where they could just touch the bottom with their heads above water.

Jim swam over to the boat, pulled out a net bag full of masks and tossed one to each of the boys. Nearly everyone on the Key had one of the big, oval diving masks. Pulling on the masks and flippers, Mike and his brothers took off into the clear, warm water. Fish darted in and out of the sea grass and the white sand bottom sparkled. The sun flickered in the water as the little waves jumped above and the boys swam in every direction.

Mike swam toward another stilt house. He pulled up, treading water and watching his dad. Suddenly, out of the corner of his eye, Mike thought he saw a huge dorsal fin moving toward him. As he turned the ominous sign of a shark had disappeared below the surface. With his heart pounding, Mike saw his dad flailing at the water and swimming hard toward him.

Then another dorsal fin came toward Mike. This fin came up out of the water and then curved back in—a dolphin. Another fin appeared, then another, and then another. The spray of mist and air came from their blowholes as the dolphins breathed. A pod of dolphins swam around Mike.

Mike took a breath and put his head in the water. As he floated, the first huge form swam under him at an unbelievable speed. His body tensed as a jolt of excitement coursed through him. He had never been this close to a dolphin before. He could feel the water press against him as it passed.

Another sleek dolphin sped right in front of Mike. This dolphin's size and power made the water swell up as it swam just below the surface. Mike had watched dolphins swim in the inlet many times, but he never realized they grew to be bigger than his dad. Mike lifted his head and took a breath.

When Mike put his face back in the water, a dolphin hovered right in front of him and peered into his mask. He reached out and touched its nose. The dolphin moved and sped away. He heard them screech and click underwater. A larger dolphin, three times Mike's size, floated next to him almost motionless. This creature, the size of the sofa in the Connelly's living room, moved slowly and gently, smiling its perpetual smile. Mike reached out and touched the dolphin's slick, smooth side. The dolphin's eye and droopy lid came within an inch of Mike's mask. The black eye evoked feelings of kindness, gentleness, and a spark of something else—a spark of something much more intense.

He thought he heard whispers: *hello…young…go…boy…shark… shark…* but he couldn't be sure. He did know that the buzzing in his head became more intense when the dolphins moved closer to him.

As his dad swam to Mike, the dolphin moved away and joined the pod circling just off the flats.

Will and Bob swam right behind their dad. "Wow, did you see that? Wow, Will!" Bob shouted, gasping for air.

"I t-touched one, D-Dad!"

"That's really cool!" Will shouted.

"Come on, boys. They're gone. Let's swim back to the boat, we've had enough excitement for one day."

Bob swam around, hoping the dolphins would return. "Stay for a minute, Dad. They might come back."

"Let's go, Bob," Jim said. Bob went back under and swam toward the boat. Jim and the boys climbed up the ladder on the dock, jumped in the boat and headed home.

Naar go with Eshu and Malak and make sure that big shark is gone, Nyla said.

Okay, Naar replied. He whistled and blasted a powerful wave of clicks in the direction of the shark. He and the other big males sped toward the deeper water.

Hovering near the bottom, the huge twelve-foot tiger shark moved in a slow circle. The shark's bulk doubled that of any of the dolphins in Nyla's pod, and it possessed a menacing and lethal weapon—multiple rows of razor sharp snaggle-teeth. The dolphins countered their arch enemy with speed, intelligence, and that special kind of sonar that humans call *echolocation*. They could hurt or even kill a shark by running into it using their noses like a battering ram. Naar, Eshu, and Malak streaked close to the shark. Feeling the dolphins' screeches and clicks, the big monster quickly moved out of the bay.

He was down on the bottom, but he's gone now, Naar said.

Good. Let's head for the Bahamas, Nyla replied.

The pod meandered toward the east.

Naar swam close to Nyla. *Wasn't that the boy who lives up the inlet?*

Yes, and I have a sense that he can hear us.

What makes you think that?

I don't know. I can just feel the presence of his mind. I have been sensing something for a while. It happens every time I swim up that inlet. You know, my mother felt something when she swam up there years ago. I have the same feeling now that I had when I came near Archie with my mother.

Naar kept swimming. He had been a young dolphin when Archie lived in the Bahamas, and Naar had never communicated with him. Back then, Naar's pod lived far to the south, around the Virgin Islands, but he had heard the stories about the great Archie Pickens. The special dolphins knew the stories of Archie as well as the legends of Captain Claire. He wondered if this little boy would be the next one to communicate with them.

At the dinner table Mike stuttered through the story of feeling the powerful dolphin swim close to him and how two of the dolphins had let him touch them. He wanted to tell his family about the whispers in his head, but he couldn't find the words to explain the mysterious phenomenon.

"You know, boys, for a moment I thought I saw a shark off to the south in the deep water. Then the dolphins' fins popped up, but it still scared me. You boys be careful and never go out there alone."

"Okay, Dad," the boys said in unison.

Mike turned to his dad. "Th-th-there *was* a sh-sh-shark, Dad."

"Did you see it?" Bob asked.

"N-no, but it w-was th-there."

"If you didn't see it, how did you know it was there?" Will asked.

Mike shrugged, picked up his fork, and played with his food.

I know, Mike thought, *I just know. I heard the word shark or maybe I felt the word shark. But I know there was a shark around. I can't prove it to them. They should believe me anyway. If I tell them about the buzzing, mom might take me to the doctor. He can't do anything. I'll keep quiet about it. It's the best thing—it's always the best thing for me. I'm sure there was a shark. The dolphins knew it, too.*

Chapter 5
Whispers

Mike shared a room with Will. Being the oldest, Bob had his own room. Mike liked the top bunk. He lay on his bed and stared down at the floor, as the moon shone through the window, and a faint ghostly glow lit the floor. Mike couldn't sleep. The sounds, the whispers from that morning, kept running through his head. He thought he heard parts of words. He knew the shark had been there, and he knew the dolphins had come because of the shark.

Mike felt a funny, faint, fuzzy sound in his head, an almost imperceptible sound, reminiscent of the sound the television made when his dad messed with the rabbit ears and lost the reception. He climbed down over the end of the bed. Rocky lay on the floor in the moonlight. Mike, in his underwear and a T-shirt, slipped out the back door and down to the boat ramp.

As a full moon glowed high overhead in a twinkling clear sky, a silvery color shaded the landscape. The breeze rustled through the coconut palms across the inlet and the water shimmered as the wind made it ripple just a little. Mike sat on the boat ramp with his arms wrapped around his legs and his knees tucked under his chin. He just sat there for a long time and stared across the inlet.

As he peered harder at the water just below his feet, something moved—an image hovered in the darkness of the nighttime water. A gray shape gently broke the surface of the dark water. A small hole opened—*Pfff!*

Hot air and spray hit him and the dolphin breathed in. Mike let out a gasp and a yelp. He pushed himself up on the concrete as the dolphin's head came out of the water and laid its chin on the boat ramp. Mike's eyes widened and he giggled with excitement. He slowly slid back down the ramp and sat next to the dolphin. He carefully reached out and stroked the dolphin's nose. *Pfff!*—air shot out again.

"H-hi, m-my n-name is M-Mike."

Nyla could hear and understand Mike. She realized he was stuttering.

Hello, young Mike, Nyla said.

Mike's eyes crinkled with amazement. He felt the sound. He felt the whispers.

... I know ... hear me ... think hard ... boy.

Mike's head throbbed with a prickly sensation similar to when his foot fell asleep. He now realized the whispers and the buzzing intensified when the dolphins came near, yet he could not grasp the significance of his feelings.

He sat for a moment, and then gasped as an idea struck him. His eyes widened even more at the thought of it, and he asked, "A-are y-you t-t-talking to m-m-me?"

Nyla slowly lifted her head out of the water and moved it up and down. Mike couldn't believe his eyes. He whispered, "A-are y-you s-s-saying y-y-yes?"

She nodded again.

"Y-yes?" His eyes bugged out and his mouth fell open—his head filled with even more static.

... hear ... let your mind ... listen ... hear me ...

The two remained close to each other for some time. The whispers became louder and the buzzing more intense. Mike rubbed his temples as his head ached a little.

Sensing Mike's discomfort, Nyla slowly slipped off the boat ramp.

She breathed and gently sank below the black water. Mike stood up and watched the pressure wave move as the dolphin slid just below the surface toward the bay. Mike jumped up on the dock and ran down through the neighbors' yards, watching the dolphin.

Good-bye, Mike, Nyla beamed out, *I'll come again.*

Nyla, what are you doing? Naar said from far out in the bay.

I am sure the boy can feel my thoughts and I want to break through to him.

Do you think he can feel the rest of us? Naar asked.

I don't think so. His mind has not become that strong, but I do believe this boy has the power.

Can the boy communicate with you in any manner?

No, he can't use his mind that way yet, but maybe he'll be able to someday. I'm going to keep trying. I am quite certain that he can feel my thoughts when I am close to him. He just doesn't understand.

Mike stood at the end of the inlet and watched the dolphins swim out of sight. He walked back to the house and noticed Rocky beside him. He wondered how long he had been there. "D-did you s-see the d-dolphin, b-boy? Y-you d-didn't bark. G-good b-boy." Rocky stood there, and tilted his head a little to one side.

The moon hung low in the night sky, and Mike knew he would be tired in the morning. Mike quietly slipped into his room and climbed up the end of the bunk bed. His brother stirred but stayed asleep. Rocky curled up on the floor. Mike tossed in his bed, wide awake. *What could it mean?* he wondered. *Why did the dolphins come to me? Why did I feel so strange? What is the meaning of the whispers?* Mike knew one thing: when he had asked that dolphin if it was talking to him, it had nodded its head 'yes'.

Mike decided not to say anything about the dolphins. He would keep it to himself. Sometimes, when kids laughed at the way he talked, it made him so mad he could cry, but he kept that inside too. The dolphins liked him and that made him happy. Mike thought it was important to keep that good, warm feeling inside. He hoped those good feelings would push out the sadness that sometimes overcame him. When he stuttered or couldn't speak, he decided to think of the dolphins. He knew that would make him feel better.

After breakfast, Mike walked out to the dock and sat gazing down the inlet.

"Mike!" His mom called, "Let's go. Time to go to school."

He picked up his book bag and ran to the house. Alice handed him his lunch box. "Get going." She lovingly swatted him on the butt, and Mike ran out the front door.

Mike sat in the classroom daydreaming about the dolphin from the night before. He always understood the lessons; school work came easily to Mike as long as he avoided talking or reading out loud. Mike raced home after school that day and sat on the dock until nightfall. But the dolphin didn't come that day.

Mike began waiting on the dock as often as he could. The dolphins came and visited him—at first just one, but then more swam up the inlet. A dim yellow light illuminated a picnic table on the dock, and Mike sat on the dock most evenings and did his homework. He liked to sit out there alone—it meant that he didn't have to try and talk, and that was okay with Mike. The sound of the water gently lapping against the pilings comforted Mike, and the sounds of dolphins breathing around the dock excited him. He felt sure that the only reason the dolphins swam up the inlet was to visit him. He just wished he knew why.

Chapter 6

Something Extraordinary

Summer arrived and school ended. Mike loved summers on the island, with lazy days of swimming, fishing, exploring the waters of the bay, and just hanging around with the rest of the kids of the Key.

Key Biscayne stretched five miles from end to end and measured two miles across. On the ocean side, the sparkling white sand beaches ran almost the length of the island. The bay side faced the city of Miami. A thick mangrove swamp grew at one end and a grove of coconut trees at the other. The village sat in the middle of the island, stretching from the ocean to the bay.

Only one passageway penetrated the mangrove swamp: the road coming from the mainland. The mangroves pressed up to the banyan trees and, in places, the road's edge. The mangrove roots bent down into the black water—long, dark, twisted fingers digging into the mud and holding up the dense trees. Visibility extended a few feet into the tangled mangroves, but beyond that darkness prevailed. Black and brown water flowed in and out and around the roots of the trees. The floor always moved, not only with the water, but also with crabs, beetles, bugs, frogs, snakes, and lizards. Rarely did any of the kids or the grown-ups venture into the mangroves, and no one ever went into the swamp at night. In the dark, the mangrove swamp became spooky and dangerous.

Growing in the water at the edge of the bay, the mangroves provided a sanctuary for many little fish living around the tangled roots—little fish always brought bigger fish and big fish brought fishermen. The marina, on the bay side, held twenty fishing boats for hire that stayed busy year-round. The kids liked to watch the boats come in with their catch. A sailfish, a marlin or a big shark always provided fun, excitement, and great stories. Many moms also showed up to buy a fresh fillet for the dinner table.

The Medina family, one of the first families to live on Key Biscayne, owned the grove of coconut trees at the other end of the island. Carmen Medina, the grandmother of the family, lived alone in the island's biggest house at the far end of the coconut grove, where she spent much of her time walking about her plantation.

An old, abandoned lighthouse stood on the tip of the island near Carmen's house. It rose out of the sand—a huge weathered brick pillar with a black iron top. Now neglected, it showed signs of its age. Ribbons of rust streaked its sides, and pieces of the black iron railing at the top hung haphazardly, twisted by the elements. A new, big, steel lighthouse now stood in shallow water in the southern part of the bay.

The Connelly boys had tied a rope to one of the palms that bent out over the inlet on Mrs. Medina's property. They nailed some wood planks to the tree next to it so they could climb up and swing out into the inlet. The boys in the neighborhood, along with Lucy Medina and some of her girl friends, would swing out and splash into the water with whoops and screams. Mike thought the girls seemed nice. They giggled and whispered a lot. Next year they would be in the seventh and eighth grades. Mike liked Lucy more than most of the other girls. She seemed to be more at ease doing things that the boys liked to do. He wished he was older.

Despite his age, the group accepted Mike as an equal. They stuck up for him when others teased him about his stuttering, yet they knew Mike could defend himself. The neighborhood kids admired Mike's toughness, inner strength, and affable nature.

On many summer days, Mike swam across the inlet and walked through the coconut trees on Mrs. Medina's property down to the cove. He enjoyed lying on the sandy beach and watching the dolphins frolic in the cove. Covering an area the size of a football field and almost hidden from the bay, the cove provided the dolphins with a calm, secure playground and rest area.

For the past year, the big dolphin, which he thought of as his friend, came to the cove with a baby swimming next to it. Mike knew it had to be the mother and her baby, because, at first, the little one never left her side. They came to the cove and the inlet often, and as time went on, the baby grew much bigger and began to stray from its mother.

On this day, as Mike stood in the water near the beach, the big dolphin bumped, pushed and rubbed against him. Other dolphins swam out in the cove but never came close to him. *Why are you here?* He thought.

Mike could hear the whispers and feel the buzzing now stronger than ever before. He thought he could hear words. … *Hello … Mike … my baby … like you …*

As the day ended Mike walked out of the water. "G-good b-bye. I h-have t-to g-go. The big dolphin rose out of the water, spun, and swam toward the bay. Mike turned and walked up the beach and into the coconut grove. Then he saw her. He quickly stood behind a palm and froze. Holding her big floppy straw hat in one hand, Carmen walked at a brisk pace away from the cove through the trees.

The open windows let in the soothing night breeze as the fan spun silently above. Rocky whimpered on the floor. Opening his eyes, Mike heard it—the faint *pfff* sound of dolphins breathing that announced their arrival in the inlet. Mike slowly climbed down and slipped out the back door, making his way through the dark to the water, with Rocky trotting faithfully along behind him. Barely moving, three dolphins floated in the inlet. Mike sat down on the ramp and put his feet in the water. He knew the dolphins had come to visit him. One of the big dolphins came over. The little one swam out in the inlet next to the other adult.

Mike heard the whispers. … *Speak to … think hard … you … learn …*

Rocky whined a little, but did not bark. The whispers tickled Mike's mind, and even as they grew louder and louder, he could not comprehend the words. The dolphin put her chin on the ramp, and Mike stroked her head.

"Th-th-thanks for b-being my f-friend." As he spoke, he bent over and rested his head against hers. Then he hugged her.

A shock wave burst through Mike's head and every muscle in his body snapped taught and tight. Throwing him up and backwards, the jolt of energy surged into Mike and slammed him against the boat sitting up on the ramp.

With a groan, Mike rolled over on the ramp. Lights flashed in his head as if he had been staring at a bright light bulb. He shivered as he clenched his hands in tight fists. He lay still, willing his muscles to relax and loosen their grip. Rocky sniffed, whined, and lay next to him.

Mike, are you hurt? Mike! Mike! Nyla swam in frantic circles.

What happened? asked Naar.

Naarin's thought was hushed. *Is the boy dead?*

No, I can feel his mind. A surge of energy flowed into him. I don't know why.

Mike slowly opened his eyes; he felt no pain, just a dullness. His T-shirt and underwear stuck to him, now damp with sweat. The dizziness made him struggle to sit up and nothing but bright white flashes filled his eyes. It took a minute or two for his eyes to focus, and he peered down at the edge of the ramp and the water. Rocky stood next to him. The big dolphin had disappeared from the ramp. Wondering how long he had been there, Mike rolled over, got on his hands and knees, and then carefully rose and started to stumble back toward the house. A dull pain ran down his neck and through his entire body.

Are you okay, Mike? Nyla sent.

He gasped, spun around, and plopped down in the grass. The tone of the words that now swirled through Mike's mind sounded like his mom's voice, but not exactly. The sound reverberated in his head, but he knew no one had spoken.

He crawled to the ramp, gasping. Could he be dreaming?

Are you okay? Are you hurt?

The words came to Mike's brain again. "I-I'm o-k-kay," Mike stammered, his stutter even more pronounced in his surprise.

Don't speak—just think.

Mike thought, *I can hear you. I can hear your words. I'm okay. I'm okay.*

That's it, Mike. Don't speak—just think.

Mike's excitement gripped him, and he could hardly get a complete lungful of air. He thought. *I know what you're saying. My name is Mike Connelly. Do you have a name?*

Yes, I am Nyla.

Mike said out loud. "N-N-Nyla"

Nyla thought, *Don't speak, Mike, just let the words come from your mind.*

The other dolphins swam over to Nyla.

I can hear the boy, Mom.

You did it. You got through to him, another dolphin said.

Yes. He can hear us. He can do it.

Voices sounding like those of a young boy and an older male came to him. The dolphins sounded like anyone on the Key—but no sound filled the air—the sound came from no direction. His excitement made him want to scream and jump in the water. *Who are those other dolphins? They can speak too?*

Yes, they have the power. They are my mate, Naar, and my son, Naarin.

Hello, I'm Naar.

Hi, The young dolphin said.

Hello, Mike thought.

Even with a whopping headache, Mike's thoughts came more quickly. *Where are you from? Do you talk to many people? How did this happen?*

Nyla thought in a concerned tone, *Mike, stay calm. How do you feel?*

My head hurts, but I guess I'm okay.

You were unconscious for a long time, Nyla said, *Can you get to your bed?*

Yeah, I'm sure I can.

Good, Nyla said. *Go lie down and try to sleep or at least get some rest.*

Naarin swam next to Nyla, *Mom, I want to talk to Mike.*

Not now, Mike heard Naar. *Your mother is right, Mike must rest, and we must go.*

Come to the cove tomorrow when the sun is high, Nyla said.

The dolphins slowly turned around in the inlet and swam toward the bay.

Mike couldn't believe it. *Please don't go. Please tell me how—why?*

Mike, I can hear your thoughts, and now you can hear mine. Don't worry. Nyla reassured Mike in a tone vaguely reminiscent of his mother's voice. *We will be back tomorrow. Please rest, your mind has had a great shock.*

What about the other dolphins? Are there other people around here who can talk to you?

Mike, go and try to sleep. We will talk tomorrow. We will answer your questions. I promise. Nyla's thoughts faded as the dolphins swam out into the bay. *Rest, you need to rest now.*

No more words came to Mike and stillness came over him, broken only by a tropical breeze rustling through the palms. He sat on the ramp and rubbed his temples with both hands. Unable to follow the dolphins down the inlet, he laid back, gazed up at the stars, and smiled. *This is the coolest thing ever,* Mike thought. *I've got to tell Will and Bob. Maybe I can get the dolphins to talk to them.*

Still a little shaky, Mike got up and crept back into his room. "W-Will, w-wake up." Mike tugged at his brother's foot.

Will turned his head out of his pillow. "Huh, what," He groaned, not opening his eyes.

Mike shoved and pushed at Will in the dark room. "W-wake up, I g-got to t-tell you s-something."

"Go to sleep," Will mumbled as he rolled over.

Mike stood there for a moment and then climbed up to his bed. *That was stupid. What was I going to tell him anyway? That the dolphins were talking to me? I better wait until tomorrow and see what happens. What if they don't talk to me again? What should I do?*

As the sun rose, Mike got up and took a bowl of cereal out to the table on the dock. He hadn't slept, but he felt energized as never before. Even though a slight throbbing continued in his head, Mike's mind raced, thinking about last night. What would he tell his mom and dad and his brothers? Could he tell Bob and Will that dolphins could speak English and that he could hear them, but no sound came out of their mouths? They would think he was crazy. How could he prove it to them? How could he show them? The more he thought about it, the more he realized he should keep this magic to himself—at least for now.

Will and Bob came out of the house. "Hey, Mike!" Bob shouted. "We're going to the Beach Club. C'mon."

Mike stared down the inlet. "I th-think I-I'll st-stay h-here."

"Mike," his mom stood at the kitchen window. "You either have to go with your brothers or come with me into town. I don't want you to be here by yourself."

Mike called back. "I-I'll go t-to the b-beach, M-Mom."

Pedaling as fast as they could, the three boys rode across the island to the Beach Club. The Club served as the private beach for the residents of Key Biscayne, and had become the most popular gathering place for the kids of the Key. Founded by the Key's early residents, the Beach Club sat on the ocean side of the Key, a little north of the newly constructed Beachside Hotel. The kids hung out in the clubroom, playing ping-pong and shuffleboard, or played volleyball outside and feasted on hot dogs, washed down with plenty of cherry Cokes. Will and Bob planned on staying at the Beach Club, and then riding over to the marina to see if any big fish had come in on the charter boats.

Mike's brothers, and some of the other kids, bobbed in the surf. Mike stood on the shore, anxious to slip away. "B-B-Bob", he shouted to his brother, "I'm g-going to the st-store f-for some i-ice c-cream!" Bob waved as Mike ran up the beach.

He sped back home, grabbed his mask, snorkel, and fins, and then jumped in the inlet. After a hard swim, he climbed out the other side and ran as fast as he could through the coconut palms to the cove, sprinting and dodging through the trees, crazy with excitement. *What if they came to the cove and then left? Maybe the whole thing is a dream. It can't be, I know I heard them, and anyway my head still hurts. I hope they're in the cove.*

He got to the beach and bent over, winded. Disappointment caught up to Mike as he stood at the edge of the flat, calm, and empty cove. After sitting on the beach for a few minutes, he put on his flippers, mask, and snorkel and slowly walked into the water. Mike thought about what he wanted to say to the dolphins as he floated on the surface. Then he heard a high-pitched screech in the water that electrified him. He thought it could be coming from out in the bay.

Where are you? Mike concentrated.

We're out here in the bay, Nyla said. *We'll be there soon.*

Mike's head filled with the clear words and his heart pounded with excitement. His mind heard Nyla perfectly, and then he heard other dolphin minds. *I don't think we should all swim into the cove.*

You, Eshu, and Corran can stay in the bay, Nyla said.

I want to talk to the boy again. Mike was sure that was Naarin.

We're going, aren't we, Mom? Another young mind asked.

Of course, dear.

Come on, Shanti, I'll race you to the cove, Naarin's mind called out.

Mike hovered in the cove, his head out of the water, and his flippers slowly moving back and forth. A huge dolphin burst out of the water at the mouth of the cove, flew through the air and flopped back with a great splash. Other dolphins followed. Mike laughed and whooped as the dolphins swam around him. He could feel the surge of the pressure waves from the powerful swimmers.

Nyla, is that you?

I'm here, Mike, along with a good many of my family.

Mike's mind overflowed as the dolphins talked to each other and to him.

Come on, Shanti, jump again.

Jump, Mom.

Watch this.

One of the dolphins flew over Mike's head.

Startled, Mike ducked. *Whoa! Watch out! Who was that?*

I'm Loa, Nyla's sister.

Another dolphin came up to Mike and balanced on its tail about halfway out of the water.

Can you do this, Mike? The dolphin asked, as it churned the water like a giant mixer. Its body rose up and the dolphin writhed backward across the cove. As its tail stopped churning, the lithe gray animal just slipped below the surface. Mike could hear the dolphin's mind laughing.

Loa swam up next to Mike. *Come on, Mike. Get a good grip on my dorsal fin.*

Why?

Just hang on.

Mike wrapped his arms around the dorsal fin of the dolphin, and then he realized what the dolphin had in mind.

Let's go! he cried.

Hold on! Loa took off so fast that Mike almost lost his grip. Water sprayed out on either side of the boy and the dolphin. Mike whooped and hollered for joy as he flew around the cove.

Okay, okay, stop! Mike let go as Loa slowed down, and then he swam over to the beach, panting from the effort of holding onto what felt like a rocket. His bare chest and stomach tingled from the friction of the water, and he had lost both of his flippers when she took off. The water came up to his waist when he stopped swimming and stood to face them. Two dolphins swam up, each depositing one of the flippers in front of Mike.

Oh wow, thanks.

Not a problem, Mike.

Nyla proceeded with the formal introductions of the dolphins in the cove.

As each dolphin said hello and talked with Mike, he realized their mind voices sounded similar to any of the voices of the people living on the Key. A peculiar thing, he thought.

His mind went wild with questions, *Where do you live?*

Risa answered him. *Here in the bay, out at sea, and around the islands of the Bahamas.*

We swim back and forth, Nyla said.

Are you related?

Oh yes. We're a pod—a family. But we have many more relatives in other pods. We're just one group. We like to swim and live together, Nyla said.

Why can I hear you?

We don't know for sure, said Nyla.

How can you send me your thoughts? Can all dolphins do this?

No, only a few of us. Mind speaking is a special power given to us by great and wonderful Teachers. There have been two other humans who have had this power. Archie died a few years ago—my father and mother knew him well. Claire lived a long, long time ago. She's a legend. We'll tell you about her some day. You, Mike, are the third human in history to hear our thoughts in your mind.

Who are your Teachers?

We can't talk about them.

Where are they?

Nyla's thoughts took on a serious tone that sounded like Mike's mother's voice when she talked to him or his brothers about something important. *For centuries, Mike, dolphins like us have sworn to keep the secret. Just know that the Teachers are very smart, kind, and gentle.*

Loa broke in excitedly, *Have you told anyone about us? Have you told anyone that you can talk to us?*

No, I didn't know what to say.

Mike, believe us, Loa now sounded a bit stern, *it is important that you keep this a secret for now.*

Mike nodded. *I promise, I'll keep the secret.*

Thank you, Nyla said. *I know you will protect us. Many of us feel that if more humans knew of our power they would try and capture us.*

I understand.

Nyla swam next to Mike and rubbed against him, *Many times, we will be around you when you are near the sea. We will try to stay out of sight and you may not know we are close to you, but as your mind strengthens you will be able to feel our presence.*

I think I could feel you today before you came into the cove.

That's good, Mike, very good, Nyla said.

Two little dolphins swam by, not paying much attention to the conversation going on around them.

Why do you have those things? asked Naarin.

To help me swim faster.

You're not a very good swimmer, Shanti said.

Loa and Nyla laughed, *You, little ones, can't walk on land.*

Who would want to? Naarin said.

Their curiosity got the better of them and the rest of Nyla's pod swam into the cove, and Mike met them and talked and played with the family through the afternoon. Mike knew his brothers would probably be wondering where he had gone, but he couldn't break himself away from this magical time. As the sun dipped down, Nyla declared that the pod needed to go.

No, please stay. Please, I have so many questions. How many are there like you? How old are you?

We'll come again soon. Don't worry. Nyla said.

Stay. One more ride.

Not today. You'll get plenty of rides, Loa said. *You must remember, Mike, we need to eat a huge amount of food to keep up our energy, and finding the fish we like takes up much of our time.*

I didn't think about that. But when will you be back? Will you be here tomorrow?

We must go back to the islands. We'll return in a few days.

Will you come to the cove?

We'll come to the inlet first, said Nyla. *Don't worry, you'll hear us.*

Goodbye.

Goodbye.

Bye now, the group said to Mike. The dolphins swam toward the entrance to the cove and out into the bay. One of the little dolphins, Shanti, jumped out of the water and spun in the air. *See you soon, Mike.* She hit the surface, causing just a ripple.

Mike laughed out loud, and decided to sit on the beach for a while.

Smiling, Carmen concealed herself behind a tree. She thought she would wait to talk to Mike about the dolphins. She had heard the whispers for years, and today the whispers filled her head as never before. Witnessing the spectacle in the cove confirmed Carmen's long-held belief that Mike possessed a magical power.

She quietly walked away.

Carmen's house on the end of the island had a wide wrap-around porch and a tin roof. The hundreds and hundreds of trees in the coconut grove hid the house from the main gate. From the bay, the house stood prominently on the southern tip of the island, where only a few palms stood between it and the sea. Guests from the Beachside Hotel often walked down the beach to the old lighthouse at the end of the island. Carmen had her caretaker, Francisco, string up a barbed wire fence to keep strangers from walking over to her house. In six-foot intervals, little red signs with white letters hung from the wire—KEEP OUT: PRIVATE PROPERTY.

Carmen, however, always enjoyed the kids of the island running through her property and playing among the palm trees. Her granddaughter, Lucy, brought friends to visit, and Carmen always made sure she had plenty of homemade coconut—and sometimes mango—ice cream on hand.

On most days, she sat under the palms near the water or on the big porch, wearing her favorite straw hat and enjoying the warm tropical breeze. With her little half-glasses perched on the end of her nose and one hand always curled around a *cafecito*, she spent much of her time reading newspapers and novels.

Lucy, the three Connelly boys, Rusty and Diane sat at a long table covered with a white table cloth that fluttered in the tropical breeze. As they ate bowls of coconut ice cream, the kids laughed and talked.

Mike struggled with idle chatter so he got up and walked with his bowl. *Where are they?* He thought. *I wonder if they are out there. Sure they are. I guess they won't come around when other people are near me. I wish they would—that would really be neat.*

Mike sat on a stone bench against the house. He heard footsteps as Carmen sat down just above him on the porch with Lucy's dad, Hugo.

"I never met him." Carmen said. "Your father went to Colombia a few times a year to meet with him. I do know that the company made a lot of money from that business."

"Now that dad is gone I've been going through the books. You're right, the money from the Colombian government has been substantial, but some of the payments don't make sense. I've got to go down there and meet this Gonzalez. He has called a few times and something just doesn't seem right."

"Be careful, your father almost never talked about him, but I don't think he liked him."

"Yeah, Dad did say a few things. I wish I knew more."

Quietly, Mike walked back to the table and got more ice cream.

Around the dome, the news of the breakthrough energized and excited everyone.

How did it happen?

He touched his forehead to mine and I believe a surge of power shot into his brain. Nyla said.

Interesting—similar incidents occurred with both Claire and Archie. You said he is eleven years old?

Yes.

He is younger than we would have liked. Do you think he will keep the secret?

I'm not sure. He stutters when he speaks out loud, and I believe him to be a quiet boy. I also sense his mind to be clear and strong.

Stay close to this young man. I'm happy that you found another contact so soon, even though he is a little young. As I have told you, the time is coming when we will need this contact.

I'll let all the dolphins know about Mike, and we'll stay as close to him as we can. Nyla chuckled as she swam away. *Too bad we can't walk on land.*

Chapter 7

Summer Reading

The dolphins told Mike that they enjoyed swimming in the cove, and Mike began sitting on the beach there every chance he got. That summer, the dolphins began to come to the cove more often—not just Nyla's pod, but many different dolphins. Nyla always explained the relationships, and it turned out that those not in Nyla's family group were always introduced as distant cousins or the closest of friends.

Swimming with the dolphins, and sitting on the beach and talking with them through his mind, became Mike's greatest joys. The dolphins asked Mike many questions about his family and friends, and his life on the island.

How many brothers and sisters do you have?

Do you like riding in a car?

What time is it?

The dolphins always asked Mike about the time. The Timex his dad had given him came in handy.

Do you like school?

How did you learn to write?

The dolphins thought writing to be a wonderful art. Mike asked the dolphins even more questions.

First and foremost Mike always asked, *How did you learn to speak?*

The dolphins never answered that question.

Where do you live?

What do you eat?

How do you sleep?

How many of you are there?

How many brothers and sisters do you have?

What do the squeaking and screeching sounds you make mean?

One night, Mike sat on his dock reading *Pinocchio*. Three dolphins swam up the inlet. As Mike saw them coming, he stopped reading and put down the book. The dolphins' minds came to him. *Mike, please don't stop reading. We love to hear you read your books.*

You can hear my mind as I read, that's amazing.

Yes, Nyla said. *Your brain is getting more powerful. When you read, you say the words in your head, and when we are near you we can hear them. Please keep reading. We love the books.*

From then on, most nights, Mike sat on the dock and read. The dolphins floated below and listened as he read the words to himself. Whenever he could, Mike walked up to Carmen's big iron gate, slipped through the fence, and walked down to the cove. And now, he never went to the cove without a book. More and more dolphins started to come—sometimes there were ten or fifteen of them swimming in the cove or just bobbing up and down in the water near the beach.

The dolphins loved the tale of *Pinocchio*. They told Mike that they knew some creatures like the wooden boy. The dolphins thought *The Call of the Wild* was an intriguing story. Many of these southern dolphins had heard of the cold north seas from some of their cousins, but only a few of them had ever been there. They asked Mike if he would read books about dolphins. Mike asked his mom, but she couldn't find any.

Mike thought it curious that the dolphins had not been back around the Key for a few days; especially since they said they couldn't wait for him to read the next chapter of *The Last of the Mohicans*.

As Mike sat on the dock reading, he saw the dolphins' dorsal fins as the pod turned up the inlet.

Nyla greeted him first, *Hello, Mike. How are you?*

Mike put down his book and stood at the dock's edge. *Hi, guys. Where have you been?*

Over in the islands, with some friends and relatives, replied Corran.

Will you read to us this evening? Naar asked. *We hoped you would read more of* The Last of the Mohicans.

Sure, but I don't remember where we left off.

We remember. Malak began to recite the last lines Mike had read to them:

"To cover! To cover!" cried Hawkeye, who just then had dispatched the enemy; "To cover for your lives! The work is but half ended."

The young Mohican gave a shout of triumph, and, followed by Duncan, he glided up the acclivity they had descended to the combat, and sought the friendly shelter of the rocks and shrubs.

Mike stood on the dock in utter disbelief. His mouth flopped open. *You remembered the exact words where we left off?*

We remember all the words, explained Malak, *we will re-tell the stories you have read to us many times, word for word.*

We carry the stories in our heads, Nyla said, *we can't carry books around. They'd get a little soggy in the ocean.*

Hehehehehe. The dolphins snickered.

That's the most fantastic thing ever. How many books can you remember?

We don't know, Corran said.

Naar rose out of the water to his pectoral fins, opened his mouth a little, and rapidly nodded his head, smiling a dolphin smile. *Just keep reading, Mike, just keep reading.*

Mike shook his head in disbelief, then turned to the exact place in the book, and began to read.

The dolphins also loved to hear poetry. They would 'ooh' and 'aah', asking Mike to read the poems again and again. Mike asked his mom to go to the library and check out books of poetry. She questioned Mike a few times about reading poetry, but she kept bringing the books. Sometimes the meanings of the poems escaped Mike, and he realized that he had to make sure that he pronounced every word correctly, because the dolphins would remember it just as he thought the words.

Mike sat and listened to Risa recite.

Ah! What pleasant visions haunt me.
As I gaze upon the sea.
All the old romantic legends,
All my dreams, come back to me …

Till my soul is full of longing
For the secret of the sea
And the heart of the great ocean
Sends a thrilling pulse through me.

The dolphins loved *Moby Dick*. They cheered when the white whale sank the ship. When Mike finished reading *Moby Dick*, Nyla said, *We have some friends who would love to hear that story. They would enjoy coming here and listening to you read it, Mike.*

Tell them to come, and I'll read it again.

Just one problem. They could never fit in this cove.

The dolphins laughed hysterically.

Do you know some giant white whales?

No, Risa said, *I don't think there are any white whales like the one in the book. But we know some very large dark gray whales.*

Can they use their brains like you?

Yes, a few of them have been taught.

What are the whales like?

They are gentle creatures and great friends. They roam the seas, and we sometimes hear them from far away.

I'd sure like to read to the whales.

Nyla joined in, *Who knows, Mike, perhaps someday you will.*

Happiness and contentment filled Mike's summer days. He knew he could read better than anyone in his class. He just couldn't say the words aloud. Now the dolphins could hear his mind, and he read to them as fast as he could. *You know, Nyla, when I talk to you I never stutter.*

Yes I know. It must be difficult for you in school and around your family and friends.

It's no big deal. I just don't say much, but I do wish I could talk to everyone else the way I talk to you.

Well, we think that there may be a few other people in the world with your power, but only a very few, and we are not sure you could communicate with each other with your minds.

That's okay, I'm just glad I can talk to you.

We are very happy as well.

The dolphins did not come every day. They told Mike they spent time out at sea and around the Bahamas. The dolphins always let Mike know when they would return to visit him, and they came to the inlet or the cove at exactly that time.

Mike asked once, *How do you tell time?*

Oh, we just feel it, Naar said, *we observe the stars, the moon, the sun, and we feel the tides. We know when the sun will go down and the moon will be bright. That's why we are always asking you what time it is. When you tell us it's four o'clock, we make a mental note of our surroundings, we feel the time, and we remember what four o'clock feels like, and we won't forget. Now we know your time.*

I could never just feel the time, Mike said. *I'd always need a watch.*

You could do it. You just have to concentrate.

Mike glanced at his silver Timex and shook his head.

Chapter 8
Sharks

The dolphins had been gone for a few days. Mike lounged in the house, thinking, while his mom folded laundry in the bedroom. Will and Bob had gone to the Beach Club that morning. They hung out a lot with Lucy and her friends. Mike always wanted to be with them. He ached to be in the middle of things—talking and laughing. But that would never be, and Mike knew it. It hurt inside. Now his new friends let him talk and laugh and read as much as he wanted. It didn't hurt so much anymore.

Mike heard a voice in his head. He recognized the high pitched voice of a young female dolphin. The voice came to him as if spoken by any one of the young girls at school.

Mike, Mike, are you there? Come quick. Help! Shanti's mind cried out.

Mike ran out the back door and down to the dock. Shanti swam frantically around the inlet.

Mike! It's Naarin. He's trapped and there are sharks. Please come quickly!

Where is he?

He's at the big lighthouse. He's trapped in a fishing net. The net's tangled in the legs of the lighthouse. He might drown. There are sharks! I'm scared of the sharks!

Where's your family?

They were behind us. We swam ahead. Now I can't find them. Come on. You've got to come now!

With all his strength Mike pushed the aluminum boat, which was leaning over on the ramp. The boat began to move. Mike pushed again and again. As soon as the back end of the boat floated in the water, it became easier to slide off the ramp.

Shanti swam around behind the boat, *Hurry, Mike. Oh, please hurry. Naarin will drown. The sharks will eat him!*

Mike got the boat into the water. He pushed off and jumped in. He stumbled to the back of the boat as it floated out into the inlet.

Shanti swam up the inlet. *Hurry, Mike!*

I've got to get the engine started.

Hurry!

Hang on. Mike pulled the rope to start the engine. Nothing happened. He pulled again and again. The engine sputtered to life. Mike grabbed the handle and sped down the inlet.

Swimming ahead of Mike, Shanti's mind screamed, *Hurry! Hurry!* She leaped out of the water, moving much faster than the little boat. Mike sped past the cove and into the channel. High tide allowed Mike to cut across the flats between the stilt houses. The new modern lighthouse with its dark gray maze of crisscrossed steel beams and iron work rose in front of him.

A high pitched whine pierced the quiet of the bay, as the little engine strained at full speed. Mike could now hear Naarin's mind crying out in a panic: *Shanti, where are you? Hurry, I can't hold up this net much longer. The sharks are all around!*

I'm only twenty tail flicks away. I have Mike with me.

Hang on, Naarin, hang on, Mike said. *I'll get you loose.*

Mike raced the little boat across the flat water. He got to one of the huge pillars of the lighthouse and tied the boat to a pipe.

Shanti swam around frantically. Barely surfacing to breathe, Naarin bobbed up and down, entangled in an old fishing net.

Mike pulled off his T-shirt and put on his mask. *Hold on, Naarin.* Not thinking, he jumped in. With his stomach churning, he knew he had to be quick.

Hurry, the sharks! The sharks are getting closer! I can't move!

Tangled among the maze of pipes that crisscrossed between the big legs of the lighthouse, the net trapped the little dolphin. Outlined against the white sand, Mike saw five, six, maybe eight sharks circling below. As he swam over to Naarin, Mike realized that none of the dark forms swimming below had focused on them—at least not yet.

Just below the surface, another large grayish brown shark swam toward Naarin and then swam away. Screeching and clicking, Naarin and Shanti's minds screamed.

Mike came up for a breath, went under, and pulled at the net around the young dolphin. Naarin kept squirming which made the mess worse. Mike went back down and struggled to pull the tangled net off the pipes. He popped to the surface realizing that he needed to cut the net away.

I'll be right back. Hang on.

Where're you going? Help me!

A knife, I need a knife.

Hurry, hurry!

Mike swam to the boat, pulled himself up on the side, and leaned in. Half in and half out of the boat, he grabbed the tackle box and opened it. Mike found the long, wooden-handled fishing knife, fell back in the water, and swam toward Naarin.

Naarin screamed again. *Shark! Shark! Help me!*

A shark had grabbed the net and chewed at it. As the shark twisted back and forth, it also became tangled in the net. Its jaw opened and closed just inches from Naarin. Luckily for Naarin, the net now kept the shark away.

Mike slashed at the shark and cut him across his snout. The shark kept gnawing at the net as blood ran into the water. Mike came up for air and gasped. He held his arm out straight with the knife in his hand, and swam right at the beast. Mike plunged the knife into the shark just below its eye.

The shark thrashed, came free of the net and, with a burst of speed, swam away. A crimson trail streamed behind him. Two of the dark forms below followed the wounded shark.

Naarin, keep still. I'll get you out. Naarin kept squirming. Mike came up, gulped for more air, and put his head back down in the water.

The blood, the sharks will be back, Naarin said.

Shanti circled the lighthouse as fast as she could. *Hurry, Mike. The sharks can smell the blood from miles away.*

Mike found the net hard to cut, but he kept sawing at it. He didn't notice the shadow that came over him, like a storm cloud blotting out the sun.

Mike, watch out! Shanti cried.

Naarin saw it too. *Oh no! Get me loose!*

I'm trying. Stop squirming.

Mike. Behind you! Naarin shouted.

Mike felt something. He turned, gasped, and almost choked. A dark gray slab of skin moved past him. Mike had never seen a shark like this. From the side, the shark appeared to be much bigger than his Dad's car—it had to be fifteen or twenty feet long. The shark bent back to look at Mike and the trapped dolphin; its eye, like a dull, lifeless, black softball, never moved. The shark's tail fin, which was as big as Mike's body, brushed against him, and he dropped the knife as the monster shark glided away.

Naarin whistled, screeched and clicked as his mind screamed. *Get me loose! Please hurry, get me loose!*

Shanti swam in circles crying. *Hurry, Mike, hurry.*

Mike came to the surface, gasped, and then, when he put his head back in the water, he saw it. The knife sat on the white sand ocean floor below him. *Shanti, go get my knife. I dropped it.*

I can't, I can't, the sharks.

Mike took a deep breath, turned down, and swam for the bottom. As the sharks circled, Mike swam between them and grabbed the knife. With his lungs bursting, he shot back to the surface, and then turned and began to saw at the net once more.

Mike churned inside as he realized that the shark had turned in the distance and now, inexorably, wove its way back toward them. Naarin and Shanti kept letting out screeches, squeaks, whistles, and clicks. As it approached, the giant shark's teeth stuck out in an eerie grin. Naarin broadcast out another high-pitched screech as loud as he could make it. The shark moved past Mike and Naarin. Mike shivered as he struggled to control his fear and confusion. He knew he could not abandon Naarin. Mike stabbed at the monster's side—the knife, and Mike's entire hand plunged under the flap of skin behind the sharks head. Wrenching back, the shark shot away, as blood gushed from the now severely lacerated gill slit.

Mike took another breath and kept cutting at the net. The shark circled again, but this time it focused on Mike and the little dolphin.

Stop squirming. I've almost got you free.

He's coming back. Hurry!

Just a little more, stay still! Mike sawed faster.

Blood streamed from its side as the shark's mouth began to open

I got it.

Mike cut through the last tangled lines holding Naarin and the little dolphin wriggled free and shot away. Mike pushed back in the water, holding the knife out in front of him.

Watch out! Watch out! Naarin screamed.

Rows of bright, menacing teeth flashed and glistened in the shark's gaping mouth. Mike peddled backward as hard as he could. Naarin darted within a fins' length of the giant shark's face and distracted him for a moment. The shark twisted toward Naarin and chased him, but then circled back toward its slower and easier prey. Naarin's lunge in front of the shark gave Mike a few critical seconds.

Mike swam to the steel leg of the lighthouse, grabbed it, and pulled himself around to the other side. The great shark slammed into the pillar and bit at the steel; then it moved around the support. Mike took a deep breath and slipped beneath its belly. A white film now concealed its cold black eye, as the shark thrashed and twisted to get at Mike, its enormous jaws opening and closing.

It happened so fast that Mike never saw the first dolphin. He heard many more screeches, whistles, and clicks, and then a loud *whump!* The huge shark writhed and bent, as its head and tail flailed back and forth. The screeching and clicking sounds of dolphins now filled the water, and a second dolphin shot up from the bottom. Mike recognized Naar, moving faster than Mike could have ever imagined. Straight up from the bottom like a writhing steel colored torpedo—*thump* —Naar rammed the shark in the belly. The shark contorted violently. Another dolphin shot at the giant and drove its nose into the shark's side. The great shark twisted so crazily that its nose almost touched its tail. As it moved away, more blood flowed from its gills and now its mouth. Two dolphins followed the wounded beast for a while. The other sharks on the bottom had disappeared.

Mike, are you hurt? A dolphin asked.

No, he never touched me.

Where are the sharks?

They're gone.

Keep searching.

Are Naarin and Shanti hurt?

No, they're okay.

Is Mike okay?

Yes, I think he's fine. He has a few cuts but he seems to be okay.

Dolphin thoughts coursed into Mike's head, as their high-pitched squeaks, screeches and clicks surrounded him. The dolphins in the group continued their echolocation clicks. They knew that most sharks moved away when they felt that many dolphins nearby. The dolphins also knew that the blood would bring the sharks back. *There is blood in the water and the sharks will not stay away for long. We must move away from this place. Let's get Mike out of the water.*

Exhausted, Mike clung to a pipe sticking out of the steel pillar. Barnacles covered the steel, and Mike had rubbed against them. Blood trickled from cuts and scrapes on his chest and arms.

Floating next to Mike, Naar said, *Here, Mike, lean on me.*

Mike put his arm around Naar's dorsal fin. Farin swam up next to him and Mike leaned on Farin as well. The two dolphins swam over to the boat with Mike between them. When Mike grabbed the side of the boat, the two dolphins swam below and gently lifted him up. He stood on their heads and stepped into the boat. Corran and Loa surfaced beside the boat.

Mike, thank you. You saved our daughter.

Naar and Nyla floated next to them. Naar spoke first, *Mike, you saved our son with an act of courage we will never forget. The sharks could have killed you.*

The two young dolphins swam close by. Naarin said, *Mom, Dad, you should have seen it. Mike stabbed one shark, but he dropped his knife. So he swam down between the sharks and got it. Then he stabbed the other big shark.*

I was so scared, Shanti added. *There were sharks all around us.*

Naarin, Shanti, many dolphins have died in the fishing nets, Nyla said. *You must be careful. You are old enough to swim on your own, but stay away from the nets.*

We were chasing some snapper when…

Quiet Shanti! Corran erupted in anger. *You two young ones should not have strayed so far away of us. You carelessly put yourselves and Mike in grave danger. If it wasn't for Mike's bravery, the sharks would have most certainly eaten both of you.*

Naarin and Shanti fell silent. Mike sat on the boat for a moment and began to calm down.

Eshu and Malak surfaced next to the boat. Eshu carried the wooden-handled knife in his mouth, and Malak had Mike's diving mask hanging over his nose.

Here, Mike, you dropped these, said Malak.

Mike didn't even remember dropping the knife again or what had happened to the mask. *Thank you.* He smiled and reached over and took the knife and mask.

Mike, you have done something we will never forget, Naar said.

Nyla's thought pushed in. *Enough, let's move away from here before the sharks come back. We will talk of this tomorrow. Mike, go home and take care of your cuts. Come to the cove tomorrow, early in the day, at your nine o'clock. Naar, follow Mike home. Make sure he's safe.*

The dolphins sank in the water and moved away. Naar stayed next to Mike's boat.

Mike pulled the cord on the engine, and this time the engine started on the first try. He swung the boat around and cruised back toward home. He thought about the great thing he had done, but he realized he couldn't tell anyone. As he came to the end of the island, he saw Carmen in her straw hat standing near her home. She watched Mike without moving or motioning and Mike kept going.

With Naar following, Mike slipped up the inlet and nosed the boat up to the ramp.

He jumped out and tugged on the front of the boat to pull it up on the ramp.

"Mike, what are you doing?"

Mike jerked his head around. Standing at the top of the ramp, his mom had her hands on her hips, and a puzzled and not too happy frown on her face. "Where have you been with the boat?"

"O-o-ut to Sti-Sti- Stiltsville." Mike stuttered even more when he told a lie. He wondered if his mom knew that.

"I came out back and found you gone and the boat missing. You worried me."

"I'm s-s-sorry, M-M-Mom."

She walked down the ramp and helped Mike pull the boat up. "You know, you shouldn't go out there by yourself. What happened to your arms and your chest? They're bleeding. What on earth happened?"

"I g-got cut by s-some b-b-barnacles on one o-of th-th-the p-piers,"

Alice shook her head. "Come inside and let me put some mercurochrome on these cuts."

Later that evening, Jim walked out to the dock where Mike sat with a book. "Mike, I know you're getting older and I know you are a good swimmer. But you shouldn't be out in the boat by yourself. I've told you and your brothers not to go out alone. Your mother became a little worried not knowing where you were."

"I-I'm s-sorry, Dad. There was n-nobody ar-r-round t-to g-go with m-me." Mike could barely get any of the words out. He so much wanted to tell his dad what he had done.

Jim decided not to push it. He sat next to Mike. "How about reading out loud to me for a while?"

"D-Dad, is it o-k-kay if I j-just read t-to m-myself?"

Jim smiled, "Sure, Mike. It's okay."

Mike watched his dad as he walked across the backyard. He knew his dad would be proud of him, if only he could tell him the story. Mike remembered his promise and he knew he had to keep the secret.

With the vision of the shark coming straight at him rolling through his mind, Mike slept very little that night. When morning came, he got up early and dressed. He sat at the table in the kitchen and ate some cereal.

Mike could not wait to get going, but knew he couldn't leave the house until his mom saw him. Mike turned on the TV and watched Roy Rogers. He walked back to his room and banged around for a while until Will stirred, and the rest of the house began to rise and shine. Alice walked into the kitchen in her long white nightgown. "Hi, Mike, did you eat something?"

"Yeah, c-cereal."

"What are you going to do today?"

Mike held a book. "I'm g-going to r-read s-some more. I've r-read f-five b-books so f-far th-this s-summer."

"I know; you've done very well. Your brothers have read only one or two." She rubbed Mike's hair.

"Mom, I'm g-going over t-to M-Mrs. M-M-Medina's to read. O-k-kay?

"Okay," she answered. "Just be home for lunch."

Mike turned to his mom. He planned on staying at the cove all day, and he wanted to spend as much time with the dolphins as he could. "Mom, w-would you p-pack me a s-s-sandwich?"

"Sure." She made him two ham-and-cheese sandwiches and put them in a brown paper bag with some cookies and a jar of lemonade. Mike grabbed the bag and his book and, with Rocky following along, made his way out the back door.

Mike ran around the inlet and ducked under Mrs. Medina's fence. With Rocky trotting a little ahead of him, Mike ran through the thick coconut grove toward the cove. As he got closer, he heard the dolphins breathing. He reached the top of the sand dune overlooking the little beach and the cove.

He gasped—his mouth fell open, and his eyes widened in disbelief as his book and lunch bag fell to the ground. Not knowing what to think, Mike walked down toward the beach. Rocky sat at the top of the sand hill, gazing out at the water. A chant rose up in Mike's head.

Mike! Mike! Mike! Mike! Mike! Mike!

In unison the dolphins cheered.

Mike! Mike! Mike! Mike! Mike!

Crowded into the cove, Mike saw what must have been more than a hundred dolphins. They floated near the shore as others moved further out in the water. The dolphins swam over, and around each other. The water teemed with shiny gray dolphin skin and triangular dorsal fins.

Mike! Mike! Mike! Mike! Mike! the dolphins chanted. Tears rolled down Mike's face. He stumbled down the beach and into the water with his sneakers on. The dolphins crowded around him as he patted and hugged as many as he could reach.

Thanks, Mike.

Great job, Mike.

You're so brave.

Thanks from all of us.

The dolphins' words ran through Mike's mind. He walked deeper into the water, up to his chest. The dolphins pushed closer.

Who are all of these dolphins?

Nyla came over to Mike and all the dolphin minds fell silent.

Mike, the dolphins here today are our family and friends. They have come from far out at sea and from the islands to honor the great, brave boy who fought the sharks. This story will be told for many of our lifetimes to come.

Smiling, Mike just stood in the water. The dolphins came around and bumped and rubbed against him, as they talked to Mike with their minds. A big dolphin swam behind Mike and put his head between Mike's legs. He lifted Mike up almost out of the water. Mike rode around the cove, waving to an imaginary crowd. The dolphins laughed at Mike's obvious delight.

After a while, many of the dolphins said good-bye to Mike and swam out into the bay. One of the large, spotted dolphins came up to the shore and flipped a big lobster out of his mouth onto the beach. *Here you go, Mike. Take this home for dinner.*

Another dolphin came up with a lobster in his mouth, spun to the side and flipped it up on the beach, then another, then another. Mike stood on the beach, his mind reaching out. *Thanks. Thanks. This is plenty. Thanks.* Before long, a pile of lobsters squirmed in the sand.

Naar swam close to Mike. *We will never forget your courage.*

Naar moved out into the cove. Eight dolphins jumped high in the air in perfect unison. At the apex of their leap they simultaneously turned their noses downward, splashed into the sea, and disappeared. Mike took off his wet T-shirt and laid it on the ground. He piled as many lobsters as he could on the shirt, and then he grabbed the edges like a bag and carried it home, leaving a bunch of lobsters on the beach.

He walked to his back door. "M-m-mom," he shouted into the house, "c-come see wh-what I g-got."

Alice opened the back door. Mike set his shirt down and the lobsters spilled out.

"Wow, Mike, where did you get them?" she asked.

"I c-caught them in th-the c-cove."

"All by yourself?" she asked.

Mike sensed his mom suspected something. "Y-yes, ma'am."

Alice smiled, "Well, we'll have some of these for dinner tonight. Your brothers will be impressed. Go get out of those wet shorts."

As she turned back into the kitchen, Mike grinned a little, relieved that his mom missed the fact that he had not taken his mask and flippers with him that day.

He went to his room, changed clothes, and sat on the floor with Rocky next to him. He thought about yesterday and today. *How can I tell anyone?* he thought as he stroked Rocky's head and back. *Jumping in the water with those sharks—that was crazy. If they knew, everyone on the Key would talk about it. I bet they would let me lead the Fourth of July parade. Mom and Dad would be mad. Bob and Will and the rest of them would think it was cool—having the dolphins throw lobsters up on the beach. They would never believe me unless they saw it. I promised I wouldn't tell. Keeping your promise—that has to be the most important thing. I guess. I just wish my brothers and Rusty and Lucy knew.*

When Mike's dad and brothers got home, they couldn't believe it. Will and Bob squawked in disbelief. "No way, Mike, no way. There have never been that many lobsters in the cove."

"Th-there w-were t-today," Mike smiled.

Jim touched Mike's shoulder, "Mike, you didn't take these out of any of the lobster traps, did you?"

"N-no, s-sir. Th-th-they were in th-the c-cove."

"Remember boys, don't go near those lobster traps. You could get arrested, or worse, if the lobster men catch up with you."

The boys smiled and nodded.

"I think the Connelly family will be eatin' well tonight," Jim announced.

After dinner, Alice dried the dishes, and the boys and their dad watched Jackie Gleason on TV. The doorbell rang. Rocky barked. Jim jumped up as Alice came out of the kitchen.

"Jim, Alice, buenas noches. Hello, boys." Carmen's voice came from behind the screen door on the front porch.

"Hello, Mrs. Medina," Jim smiled.

"Hello, Carmen," Alice said, "come on in."

As usual Carmen wore her straw hat and she carried a book in one hand and a canvas bag in the other. "I found this book under a palm. I thought it must be Miguel's." She handed Mike his copy of *The Swiss Family Robinson*.

"Thanks," Alice said. "Mike, aren't you going to thank Mrs. Medina?"

"Th-thank you, m-ma'am," Mike glanced at her. She stared back and smiled. Remembering where he had dropped the book and his lunch bag, Mike realized that Mrs. Medina hadn't found the book under a tree. Mike wondered; his mind raced. *She found the book on the sand dune. I dropped my lunch bag too. She didn't bring it back. Why?*

"Oh, Alice," she motioned at her bag, "My man, Francisco, caught a bunch of lobster today along the seawall. I brought you some." She handed Alice the canvas bag.

Carmen's words slapped Mike. He fought to stay calm. *The lobsters I left on the beach. She brought them to me. How did she know they were mine? She knows. She must have seen me with them.*

Alice smiled, "Well, that's interesting. Mike just brought home a bunch that he caught over in your cove. I hope you don't mind."

"Of course not. The children are always welcome."

Mike paid no attention to the television. He watched Mrs. Medina as she walked into the kitchen with his mom. She turned back over her shoulder and held Mike's gaze for a few seconds.

The two women sat at the kitchen table and drank coffee. They talked about the island. They talked about Carmen's son, Hugo, and his wife, Amparo, and their daughter, Lucy. Alice talked about the boys and the drugstore.

Carmen sat for a while. Mike pretended to watch TV. He wondered whether she could hear the dolphins with her mind. He stared at Mrs. Medina and thought hard, *Mrs. Medina, can you hear me?* She never moved.

She can't hear me. The dolphins said I was the only one. Maybe she can feel them.

Standing, Carmen said good-bye. Alice thanked her for finding Mike's book and for bringing the lobsters. As Carmen walked to the front door, she stopped. "Boys, come by and visit me. I have lots of ice cream."

Will and Bob turned away from the TV. "Yes, ma'am," they both said, with a pair of big grins. Carmen paused in front of Mike. "Miguel, when you come to read in the grove, stop by the house. I'll give you something to drink."

"Th-thank y-you."

Carmen gazed at Mike for what he thought to be a long time. "Good night, Jim, good night, Alice," she said, as she walked down the front path.

Chapter 9
The Beach Club

The next day, Mike went to the Beach Club with his brothers. Mike wanted to go to the cove, but his mom insisted that he go with his brothers. As soon as they arrived, a volleyball game started. Mike didn't play. He wandered down the beach past the villas of the Beachside Hotel.

When the kids weren't playing games, they hung around the snack bar at the Beach Club. The round cement tables and benches buzzed with young people drinking cherry Cokes and Orange Crush. The exuberance of this spot and the smell of grilling hamburgers always drew a crowd of Key kids.

As Mike walked back toward the club, he saw Lucy dragging an inflatable canvas raft behind her. He broke into a run. "Hi, L-Lucy."

"Hi, Mike, what are you doing?"

"Oh, n-nothing. N-Neat r-raft."

"Yeah, my dad got it for me yesterday." Lucy walked into the water. "Come on."

Mike ran into the waves. The two bobbed up and down twenty yards off shore and Mike grinned as he held onto one side of the raft across from Lucy. He couldn't believe his good fortune.

Ben Hampton, the lifeguard, sat up on his white platform with a big blue umbrella tilted toward the sun. He wore sunglasses and had white zinc oxide smeared over his nose and cheeks. Pointing and yelling, Ben stood. "Dolphins!"

Out in the ocean, about fifty yards beyond Mike and Lucy, dorsal fins rolled out of the water and then back below the surface.

Lucy turned and saw the gray form for a moment, and then, right in front of her, a big dolphin popped up. *Pfff.*

Lucy gasped and Mike just laughed.

Hello. Are you Mike?

Yep, who are you?

I'm Tobias. You don't know me, Mike. I live over in the Bahamas. I only come over here once in a while. I wanted to meet you—the brave boy who fought the sharks.

That's me.

Great, Tobias said. *Let's have some fun. Who is this?*

She's my friend, Lucy.

Tobias laughed. He swam next to Mike. Mike grabbed his dorsal fin.

"C-come on, L-Lucy."

Lucy hesitated.

"It's ok-kay," Mike smiled, "c-come on."

Lucy swam over and put her arms around Mike's neck. The two flew away with Mike holding on to the dolphin, and Lucy holding on to Mike. Water sprayed up around them, and they began to laugh hysterically.

Slow down! Slow down! I'm losing my grip.

Just hang on tighter. I only have one speed—faster than a barracuda.

Lucy slipped off Mike's shoulders and grabbed his bathing suit, almost pulling it off. Mike let go of the dolphin, as he blushed beet red and the two continued to laugh and giggle as they bobbed up and down in the water. Mike now felt the big dolphin below him. The dolphin's head slipped between his legs. Then, with a big push, Mike flew in the air, arms and legs going every which way. Another dolphin came up under Lucy. She screamed as she was tossed in the air. They both splashed down and then went flying again.

Everyone at the beach club gathered at the water's edge and watched in amazement, cheering and shouting. Hoping for a ride or a toss, many of the kids swam out to where Mike and Lucy hung on the raft. As the other kids came close, the dolphins disappeared and Mike heard a chuckle in his head and then, *See you around, Mike.*

Lucy and Mike came to the shore, pulling the canvas raft. A crowd gathered around as Lucy babbled a mile a minute.

"Did you see that?! They came right up to me and Mike. Did you see them? They were so cool! What a blast!"

Excited, Mike knew he couldn't talk about what just happened, so he remained quiet. He thought about Lucy with her arms around his neck. *If only she knew why the dolphins came.*

Ben, the life guard, walked over to them. "Wow, kids, that was amazing." Ben put his hand on Mike's shoulder. "There are always lots of dolphins in these waters, and I'm telling you, I've never seen anything like what just happened to you two."

Rusty and Bob stood next to Lucy.

"How did you get them to do that?" Rusty asked.

"I don't know," Lucy said, "one of the dolphins let Mike grab onto its dorsal fin."

Mike shrugged and smiled.

Mike noticed two men dressed in long pants and white guayaberas standing over on the Beachside Hotel property, watching intently.

The crowd broke up and Lucy and Mike walked away from the water with Lucy dragging her raft.

"You know, I think those dolphins like you."

"Yeah, I g-guess s-so" Mike smiled.

The two men walked along the chain link fence separating the hotel from the Beach Club. *The excitement is over,* Mike thought. *Why are these men still watching and following us?*

That evening at dinner, Will and Bob told the story about Mike, Lucy, and the dolphins. Jim said, "Oh, I heard about it at the drugstore. Mr. Gould came in and told us all about it. He said quite a big crowd gathered on the beach. Were you scared, Mike?"

"N-no, th-the d-dolphins just w-wanted to p-play."

Alice said, "You know, boys, the dolphins swim up the inlet quite a bit. You should try to play with them near the dock some time."

Mike wondered how many times the dolphins had come to the inlet to visit him and listen to him read a book, and found that he wasn't on his dock. Being near the dolphins was more important than anything in his life.

Chapter 10

He'll Fight Another Day

Every year, in late August, Hugo Medina, Lucy's dad, took her and some of her friends out on his big yacht for a few days. They cruised to the Bahamas to snorkel, swim, and fish. This year, Mike, his brothers, and his dad were going. Bob and Will had been on this annual excursion before, but this was Mike's first trip. Mike's friend, Rusty, his sister, Diane, and their dad, Paul, would also be along. Counting Lucy's friend Clara, there would be seven children and three adults.

The sleek white-and-chrome, seventy-foot yacht had the words *Las Olas, Key Biscayne, Florida* emblazoned across the back in gold letters. The railings around the aft fishing deck stood only four feet above the water, to make it easier to pull fish into the boat. Where the gate in the back wall of the fishing area swung open, a wooden grate could be unfolded down into the water. When the boat stopped, the passengers could swim off the back of the boat and climb back on with no trouble. The boys also thought the wooden platform to be a great place to stand and pee in the ocean—when they went out without the girls, of course.

Two swiveling "fighting" chairs, for bringing in big sailfish or marlin, sat bolted near the middle of the fishing deck. They resembled wooden barber chairs equipped with special chrome rod holders attached to the fronts of the seats, with wooden footrests for maximum leverage.

Forward of the rear fishing platform, two steps led up to the main cabin. Dark blue couches lining the sides hid storage bins containing orange life vests and other gear. A U-shaped counter enclosed the galley located in the forward starboard corner of the main cabin. Next to the galley a stairway went down to the main stateroom, where the girls would sleep. The dads would use the smaller cabins below on either side of the stairs. The boys had staked out the main cabin for themselves. Underneath the stairs and to the rear, a small dark green steel door separated the engine room from the rest of the yacht.

Used in bad weather, the inside cockpit stretched across the width of the yacht, a step above, and forward of the main cabin. Most of the time Hugo drove the boat from the outside cockpit over the main cabin. It was accessible by an outside ladder from the lower fishing deck. Aluminum scaffolding rose above the yacht, and supported a platform just large enough for one person to stand, with yet another set of controls. From this vantage point a captain could find weed lines, and birds feeding on bait fish, indicating where the big fish might be.

In the darkness of early morning, the families converged on the dock next to the Medina house and loaded supplies, food, and equipment onto the boat. The two picnic baskets, packed by the ladies, received the most attention. Smells of fried chicken, freshly-baked biscuits, cookies, and brownies seeped out of the baskets. The boys started to dig into them before the boat pulled away from the dock. Amparo Medina called, "Girls, pack as much of that in the fridge as you can."

Jim shooed the boys away from the baskets. "Boys, we've got to make this good food last, or we'll be eating a lot of peanut butter."

As dawn broke, *Las Olas* pulled away from the dock. The kids and dads waved good-bye to the moms standing on the dock. Pulling around the island and past the stilt houses, the yacht headed out to sea.

The big fishing boat trawled into the dark blue water of the Gulf Stream. Four fishing lines ran out from *Las Olas.* Paul Butler and Jim talked about how big sailfish and marlin sometimes traveled along the edge of the imperceptible stream; but no one had any luck, so they pulled in their lines. Hugo drove from the cockpit above the main cabin. He sped the boat up, and the diesel engines roared as the boat headed east.

Around eleven o'clock, Paul brought out a platter of fried chicken, coleslaw, and biscuits for the group. As the kids ate, they talked about the islands and school. Lucy, Clara, Rusty, and Bob, now going into the eighth grade, would have a new teacher in the fall. Diane and Will were moving into the seventh grade. Mike would be in the sixth. Diane and Will teased him about getting Mrs. Aronsen.

"We had her last year," Diane said. "She is the toughest teacher in the school."

"Yeah, I think I got wacked with that yardstick every day," said Will.

"That's because you were always talking," Diane said.

"W-well I d-don't t-talk m-much."

Diane and Will both smiled and nodded.

As the big cruiser glided along, Hugo pointed from the bridge, "Hey look! Dolphins!"

Eight dolphins skipped along the surface, riding on the wake pushed out by the bow of the yacht. Swimming parallel to, and leaping ahead of the boat, the dolphins let the wake catch them, and then they bodysurfed the wave.

Paul stood against the side rail. "See that kids, the dolphins are riding in our wake."

"Why do they do that?" Clara asked.

"Some people think they do it when they find a boat traveling in the same direction that they are going. Riding the wake makes it easier for them to swim—it's like riding a surf board. I think the dolphins do it just for the fun of it."

The kids and dads leaned over the sides of the boat, watching the dolphins. Mike propped himself on the back railing of the boat, wondering if any of these dolphins could hear his mind. Mike's head filled with words.

Hello, Mike.

Pike, is that Mike, the young shark fighter?

Yep. Sure is.

Mike heard the minds speaking in his head. He began to smile. None of the other kids noticed.

Hello, Mike. I'm Salvador, the dolphin said, *I've heard about you and your battle with the sharks.*

Hello, Mike said.

Hi, Mike. I'm Pike, where are you going?

Over to Nassau and around the islands for a few days.

Great. We're sure to bump into you again. Pike said.

Do you know Nyla and her family?

Of course we do, said Pike.

Are they over in the islands?

I don't know, said Salvador. *But if we run into them, we'll tell them you're over here for a visit.*

By just slowing down a little and falling back behind the boat, the dolphins disappeared.

Hey, Mike, Salvador said. *You should fish around here. There are big sail-fish in these waters.*

"M-Mr. B-Butler, let's f-fish some m-more."

"Good idea." Paul yelled up to Hugo in the cockpit, "Hugo, slow it down. We're going to put out some lines again."

The engines stopped roaring as the big boat slowed. Jim climbed down from the bridge, and Hugo climbed up the ladder to the controls in the top tower, high above the boat.

"Let's go for a big one, kids!" Jim shouted.

"Who wants a rod?" asked Paul.

Mike plopped down in one of the teak fighting chairs. "C-c-can I t-t-try?" he asked.

"Sure, Mike," Paul put a big rod in the round steel holder at the base of the chair. Mike positioned one leg on either side of the rod. His feet rested on the wooden footrest.

Mike grabbed the rod. He felt pretty good sitting there. Lucy sat in the chair next to him. The other kids grabbed rods and stood on the sides. The men hooked lures to the lines and put them in the water. With all the fishing advice from the dads, the kids felt sure they would catch the big one.

"Okay, let out a lot of line," Paul said. "Make sure your drag is set. And remember, don't jerk on the rod if something hits. Just let the fish take it and run."

The kids watched their fishing rods and gazed out at the sea behind them as the boat moved slowly through the water. Diane and Bob sat on the side rails of the boat. They trolled for a time and Mike began to doze a little.

Salvador's words hit Mike: *Hey, Mike, get ready.*

Mike jerked to attention and took a deep breath. He sat up and grabbed the rod a little tighter. Lucy turned and stared at Mike.

Where are you? Mike asked.

We're back here following a big fat sailfish and kind of pushing it your way, Pike said. *You know, this fish is so fat it might be a tuna. Hehehehehe.*

The high pitched chattering laugh of the dolphins made Mike smile. He noticed Lucy's puzzled gaze out of the corner of his eye.

I told you that some big sailfish swim around here, but Mike, Salvador said, *you have to promise me that if you catch this one, you'll let it go.*

Pike jumped in, *We don't mind humans fishing for food, and we understand why you like to hook these big fish.*

We like to play with them too, said Salvador.

But, Pike said, *we believe catching one of these great fish, pulling it out of the water, and killing it just for the sport of it is a crime against all the creatures of the sea.*

I understand. If I catch it, I'll let it go. I promise.

Hugo shouted down from the tower, "Big weed line over there!" He pointed off to the rear. A few moments later Hugo yelled down again, "Bill fish!" But no one down below caught sight of the sailfish.

Mike's rod nearly jumped out of his hands. He grabbed tight and gasped as it bent. Everyone paused. Nothing happened, and the rod straightened. A few seconds passed. The rod bent over again, and this time the reel screamed to life. *Wheeeeeeeee*—the line pulled out so fast that the spinning reel made a sound like a small siren.

Hugo stopped the boat and began to shout down instructions. "Jim, Paul, bring in the other lines. Mike's got a big one."

"Let's go, kids," Paul said, "we don't want your lines tangled with Mike's."

"Hurry, kids, get those lines in faster!" Jim said.

The men were more excited than the kids. Jim helped Lucy. Paul stood next to Mike. As the reel spun and screamed, Mike held the rod with a tight grip. Paul splashed some water on the reel to cool it down. Then he hooked the leather straps hanging from the chair to the rings on either side of the reel.

"Can you hold on, Mike?" his dad asked.

"Y-y-yeah, I g-got h-h-him."

With the other lines pulled in, the kids gathered around Mike. Paul reached over and twisted the knob on the side of the reel. "Mike, I'm tightening the drag on your reel. It'll slow this big fish down."

Mike's dad came up behind him. "Put your hands as high up on the rod as you can."

Jim knelt down on one knee next to his son. "Now, use your legs and pull back on the rod. Then rock forward and reel in with your right hand."

Following his father's directions, Mike kept pulling and reeling, pulling and reeling, even though each backward pull got harder.

The kids cheered him on.

"Come on, Mike!"

"Get him, Mike!"

"Keep pulling!"

Lucy sat next to Mike and watched intently.

Paul said, "Okay, pull as hard as you can, Mike. You won't lose it."

The rod bent over and the reel whined as the line went out again. Mike kept hanging on.

Sweating in the baking sun, Mike continued to pull on the rod and reel in the line. From time to time, the fish pulled the line out again. Mike thought he might not be gaining any line, but he kept pulling, determined to catch this great fish. As the battle dragged on, the kids stopped cheering and sat around Mike.

His arms, legs, and back ached, and Mike began to wear down as the sweat dripped off him. He saw his dad and Paul glance at each other, and he knew they were wondering if he could win this battle.

Mike heard Salvador. *Hey, Mike, you're doing great. This fish is getting tired.*

I'm pretty tired too, I don't know if I can keep going.

You can do it, said Pike.

Where are you?

We're just out here watching. This is a big fish, and you're going to catch it. Just remember, you have to let it go.

I will.

Mike felt the line go slack.

"Crank it, Mike," Paul encouraged him.

Mike reeled as fast as he could. The great fish blasted out of the water fifty yards behind the boat. The shining monofilament line led from the fish's mouth down into the ocean and then back to the tip of the rod. It shook its head violently in an attempt to throw the hook from its mouth. Twisting, squirming, and turning, the fish partially rose out of the water. It moved across behind the boat and then fell back into the sea.

"Oh my God," Jim said. The kids screamed and pointed.

Paul said, almost to himself, "That fish is at least a hundred pounds."

Jim knelt next to his son, "Are you okay? Can you do it?"

Mike gritted his teeth and nodded his head, as the reel continued to scream.

The spear-like nose of the sailfish slashed back and forth. Then it disappeared. Now, thirty yards behind the yacht, the pointed nose broke the surface. The powerful yet lithe animal rose up again, only its tail still in the water.

The dark blue of its topside blended to lighter blue and then aqua down its sides. Underneath it shone like silver coins. The ribbed dorsal fin on its back fanned out.

Thrashing back and forth behind the boat, the sailfish flailed at the water in a contorted dance atop the ocean. It slapped down with a mighty splash. Mike had heard the captains at the marina talk about these fish and the fact that they would keep fighting and never give up. Mike's face now grimaced with pain every time he pulled back on the rod.

Standing on either side of the chair, the men grabbed the rod, each with one hand, and started pulling. Jim smiled at his son, "Mike, you just reel it in. It's your fish. Paul and I are going to help you a little. You know this sailfish is probably twice your size."

Mike nodded, happy that the two men now helped him with his great battle.

The men pulled, and Mike turned the reel. As he reeled he wondered if the sailfish hurt as bad as he did. Now, twenty feet from the *Las Olas*, it appeared that the sailfish had begun to give up. But as it got closer to the boat, it still twisted and splashed. The kids screamed with glee.

"Wow!" Rusty yelled. "It's almost longer than the back of the boat."

"Its colors are so bright," said Carla. "I've never seen colors like this one has."

"When they are pulled out of the water and die they lose a lot of their color," Paul said.

"I don't think I've ever seen one come in at the marina as big as this one," Will said. "Way to go, Mike."

Climbing down and joining the rest of the excited group, Hugo grabbed some thick leather gloves, a short wooden pole with a big nasty hook on the end of it, and some rope. He unhooked the steel leader from the rod and held the line to the fish in his gloved hand. Mike put the rod down and stepped to the rail next to his dad. "D-Dad, I w-want to l-let it g-go."

Mike's dad, Paul, and Hugo turned to Mike. As the fish had their full attention, the kids missed what Mike said.

"Are you sure you want to let him go?" Hugo said, "It's a monster fish."

"Y-yeah. I d-don't want t-to k-kill it,"

Hugo put the big hook down. "Jim, get me the big needle-nose pliers out of the box."

Jim got the pliers and gave them to Hugo. Exhausted, the fish stopped struggling to get free, but managed to splash water on everyone at the back of the boat. Paul held onto Hugo's belt from the back so he wouldn't fall in. Hugo twisted the hook with the pliers, and it popped out of the fish's mouth. The kids cheered, not realizing what had happened.

"He's getting away! He's getting away!" Bob shouted.

"Get him dad!" Lucy yelled.

Sitting motionless for a moment, the great sailfish rolled to one side and then dove out of sight.

Hugo shouted, "Adios, amigo! You live to fight another day." He turned to Mike. "Thanks to you, Mike." Hugo patted Mike on the shoulder.

Mike's dad touched him on the head. "Great job, Mike, that was one of the biggest sailfish I've ever seen."

Mike remained quiet, as everyone else talked about the great adventure. A dolphin's words came into Mike's head. *You did the right thing, Mike.*

Exhausted, Mike sat back down in the fighting chair and smiled at Lucy. She sat in the other chair with that same puzzled expression on her face. Mike wondered what she was thinking. He hoped she was proud of him.

Chapter 11
Nassau

With the sun high behind her, *Las Olas* cruised into Nassau Harbor. The light-blue clear water always amazed visitors to these islands.

Rows of shops and buildings lined the waterfront, painted with dazzlingly bright colors. In Nassau, a banana-yellow house might have bright blue shutters, or a cherry-red house might have yellow or green shutters. The colors of the buildings matched the colors of the bright parrots and macaws that flew around the islands.

Most of the shops had no front doors; the merchants folded back shutters opening their stores to the street. Straw hats and baskets, strings of white and pink shells, and brown sponges hung in the shops and spilled out onto the sidewalk in cluttered displays. On the streets, white and tan canvas tops held up by poles flapped in the breeze and shielded even more goods, steaming pots, and smoking grills from the blistering sun.

Drinking a Coke, Mike sat on one of the teak chairs watching the sights of Nassau. Letting the sailfish go made Mike happy, even though his body ached. He wondered what his dolphin friends would think. Hugo guided the boat toward a vacant dock. Paul positioned himself at the stern, and Jim stood at the bow, with ropes ready to tie to the big posts on the pier. Jumping off onto the wooden planking, Paul tied his rope to a post. Then he ran to the front and Jim threw him the other line. The engines stopped rumbling below, and the kids scrambled up onto the dock.

"Let's go," Lucy said, "there's all kinds of stuff to see and do."

"Y-y-yeah, l-let's g-go."

"Kids," Paul announced, "no one can leave this dock until the adults are ready to go with you. It will take us just a few minutes."

Two men with shiny mahogany colored skin walked down the pier side-by-side. They wore white coats cinched at the waist with a dark blue belt. Their white coats, dark blue pants with a red stripe down the side, and gold braids covering the brims of their dark blue hats, gave them the appearance of members of a very spiffy marching band. The two officials stopped to talk to Paul.

Paul turned to the boat. "Hey, Hugo." He pointed to the two men. Hugo waved at them. The officials stepped aboard. Hugo showed the two uniformed men some papers, and the Bahamians smiled, shook hands with Hugo, and stepped back onto the dock.

One of the men walked over to the kids, and gave them a wide, white, toothy smile. "You children be careful now and have some great fun," he said in the lilting speech of the Islands.

The other official turned to the two dads. He smiled, "Welcome to Nassau."

The men finished putting away the fishing gear. *Las Olas* would spend that night and the next morning in Nassau.

"I want to go to that shop we went to last year," Diane said.

"My mom said I could get one of those dresses," Clara said. "Let's all try to get one."

"How are you feeling? Will asked Mike.

"G-good."

"You've got to be hurting after that fish."

"Y-yeah, b-but j-just a l-little."

The group walked down the pier and onto the main street of Nassau.

Lining the street near the pier, horses pulling brightly-colored wagons with canvas tops waited for tourists to hire them.

Diane pointed as they got closer. "Look at the straw hats on the horses."

"Yeah," Will laughed, "with their ears poking through."

The kids ran toward the horses. "This one has ribbons." Lucy rubbed the brown horse's nose.

"Welcome to Nassau," the man sitting atop his open buggy said. "This fellow can pull you around town real easy now. How about a ride?"

"Thanks, not right now." Jim said.

As the dads and kids walked, they enjoyed the exotic aromas of fruit, fish, and flowers coming from the shops and stands along the street. The shopkeepers smiled and laughter filled the air. On the main street, big black pots containing rice and beans boiled. Fish, conch, and skewers of shrimp cooked on the grills. The smoke and smells floated on the breeze and, along with the colors and sounds, filled Mike's senses.

A gray-haired man sat amid piles of green and light brown coconuts, working hard at husking them. Next to him, a wooden table held a few peeled brown nuts with drinking straws poking out of the tops. Mike and Will stopped for a moment and watched the man. As he worked he sang a little song:

"Ya drink da fresh cool coco milk ya feel good all da day.
Ya drink da fresh cool coco milk it drive da heat away.
Ya drink da fresh cool coco milk an mix it whit da rum.
Ya drink da fresh cool coco milk an have da island fun."

Mike thought living here must be like being part of a constant backyard barbecue.

Other vendors spoke out in their island way, "Hello, young man. How about a hat?"

"Would you like something, boys?"

"You'd look mighty fine in this shirt."

"Good morning, young ladies."

Lucy, Clara, and Diane found a shop with dresses in colors brighter than anything at home. Hugo stayed with them as the girls chatted with each other and flipped through the racks of dresses.

The boys kept walking down the street. They slipped in and out of the shops, moving back and forth across the street.

Mike and Will turned down a narrow cobblestone alleyway. Shutters were closed over some of the windows in the alley. Other shutters hung haphazardly off the buildings, waiting to fall at any moment. No car, or even a horse and buggy, could fit up the narrow way. The buildings on either side tilted toward each other. Wires stretched above and laundry hung, drying in the tropical breeze.

The boys walked into a dark shop with hundreds of baskets, hats, and bags stacked on tables, hanging about, and dangling from the ceiling. The shop smelled of straw, a strange, earthy smell.

A big woman walked from the back of the shop wearing a loose-fitting yellow dress, which flowed to her ankles. Wrapped around her head, she wore a bright scarf of red, blue, and green, which, held in a great amount of hair.

"Hello, boys. Where are you from?" She asked with a big smile.

"We're from over by Miami, on Key Biscayne," Will said.

"Ah, that's a beautiful place, but not as pretty as these islands, eh, boys?"

"Yes, ma'am, It's real pretty here."

Not saying anything, Mike smiled and wandered deeper into the dark shop. He stared through the maze of straw items and noticed some light coming from the far end of the room. Bright blotches of color began to emerge through the piles of goods hanging off the tables.

He pushed past the straw and walked to a wall covered with the most striking paintings he had ever seen. Shining down from the ceiling, beams of light caused the colors to jump out at him. Mike gazed up at what must have been a hundred pictures, from the size of the table top in his kitchen to the size of his hand. In front of the display, more paintings mounted on white mat board stood upright in cardboard boxes, so customers could flip through them.

Mike recognized that the people, buildings, and scenes in the pictures portrayed Nassau, the islands, and the island people, but the colors screamed out in an exaggerated bright and vivid fashion. After staring at the pictures for a while, Mike decided that the brilliant colors gave the pictures their unique beauty. The lady in the yellow dress walked up next to Mike. "It is truly lovely island art. I could stand here and look at it all day long."

"Y-yes, m-ma'am, m-me too."

She smiled. "Well, you just enjoy yourself." She wandered away into the shop.

Far up the wall, almost at the ceiling and off to the right, Mike saw the painting. It pulled him in and he couldn't take his eyes off of it. Two neon-green dolphins flew out of the water against a cloudless blue sky. The bright colors burst off the canvas.

Oblivious to the time, Mike stood there staring at the painting, mesmerized.

"So, do you like the paintings, young man?" a voice boomed out.

Almost jumping out of his skin, Mike spun around. A man with twinkling brown eyes stood beside him. His teeth shone bright white against his ebony face. Big tangled braids like thick, black hunks of fuzzy rope poked out of his head in every direction. He wore an old, stained T-shirt with blotches of color all over it. A pair of dark blue pants, held up by rope at the waist, sported even more smears of bright paint. The frayed pants hung down, touching the floor. His toes stuck out of brown sandals.

"Y-yes, s-s-sir,"

"Ahhh, yes, they are pretty," the man smiled.

The woman in yellow walked over. "Mr. Crain, how are you?"

"Fine, Miss Safiya, fine. What's new?"

"Oh, not much. Some of your fine paintings sold this week. I wasn't expecting you so soon."

Mike stood there, almost between them.

"Oh, I was just stopping by."

"This young lad has been admiring your work."

"D-did you p-paint all of th-them?"

"Well, it is my work," The man smiled.

Mike pointed up, but before he could say which one he liked, the man interrupted, "The green dolphins. That's a good one."

The man walked over to one of the cardboard boxes, and he began flipping through the paintings. Mike noticed that the artist had a curious lump sticking out next to his pinkie finger on both of his hands. The disfiguring lump protruded from the base of his pinkie finger and extended almost to his wrist.

"So, young man, what is your name?"

"M-M-Mike C-Connelly."

"Well, Mike, I'm Wilson Crain, and this is for you." The artist pulled a matted painting from one of the boxes. A mirror image to the painting hanging above, green dolphins jumped against a vibrant blue background. Gingerly, Mike took the picture.

"Th-thank you. Th-thanks a l-lot."

"You're welcome, young Mike."

Mr. Crain's eyes conveyed a strange kindness, but Mike felt uneasy. He turned and ran out of the shop. Stopping in the narrow alley, Mike looked up and then down the street, and saw Will, Bob, Rusty, and the two dads walking toward him. Mike ran up to them.

"Look w-what I g-g-got," Mike held up the painting.

His dad took the painting, "Where did you get this, Mike?"

"A m-man gave it t-to m-me."

"Where is he?"

Mike pointed, "In th-that sh-shop."

Mike and his dad walked ahead with Paul and the other boys behind them.

Miss Safiya sat on a wooden stool out front. "Hello again young man. Thanks for bringing me some customers," she grinned.

Jim smiled. "Hello. Did someone here give this to my son?"

"Oh, yes, Sir. Wilson Crain, the artist, gave it to him, and what a delightful boy you have." She smiled at Mike.

"Thank you. Is he here?" Jim asked.

"No, sir, he just walked up the street," she pointed. "It's no problem. Mr. Crain gives away pieces of his work from time to time. Come on in and wander around my shop."

Jim and Paul both smiled. Paul nodded at Miss Safiya and then at the boys. "Okay, boys—get in there and pick out hats for yourselves."

As they ran into the shop, Miss Safiya slid off her stool, and followed the boys.

The boys soon reappeared, sporting their new hats woven of light tan palm fronds with colorful bands of cloth tied around them. The boys immediately convinced themselves that they now wore the neatest hats on the island. They wandered around the little streets of Nassau until the sun started to set, and then they headed back to the boat. Mike walked behind the others, staring at his little painting. He thought about the dolphins and about Mr. Crain.

Already aboard, the three girls wore their new island dresses. The dresses flowed to their ankles and had puffy sleeves, curved necklines, and thin white leather belts.

As the girls stood together, Mike thought the fire engine red, banana yellow, and electric blue dresses resembled one of the colorful paintings he had seen earlier. "Y-You all l-look g-great."

As the sun dipped below the horizon, Nassau Harbor began to reflect the peaceful quiet of the evening. The dads set up a charcoal grill on the dock and cooked hamburgers as they stood around enjoying a little island rum. The kids ate while they sat along the edge of the pier.

"That big sailfish sure was neat," Diane said.

"Yeah," Will said, "I don't think there has ever been a bigger one brought in at the marina."

Mike grinned a little and kept eating.

Clara stood up and motioned back behind the boat. "That fish, dancing on the water… that was something I'll always remember."

"We should have pulled him in and taken some pictures," Will said.

"Hey, Mike," Bob asked, "how come you let him go?"

Mike sat silently. Hugo broke in, "He was almost too big to get aboard. Anyway, Mike caught him and Mike wanted to let him go."

Mike smiled and shrugged. He knew he had done the right thing—he had kept his promise.

As it grew dark, the boys decided to take the cushions off the couches and sleep out back on the open deck.

Mike sat on the couch up in the outside cockpit. He thought he would sleep there. Mike always liked the solitude and the quiet. Then he heard someone climbing up the ladder. Lucy pulled herself up and sat down.

"Hey, Mike, I've got to ask you something. Today, just before the sailfish hit, you kinda jumped up and tightened your grip on the rod—like you were getting ready. But I know you couldn't have seen that fish. So how did you know?"

"I j-just f-felt it."

"What do you mean, just felt it?"

Mike shrugged.

Lucy shook her head and then slowly went back down the ladder.

Mike thought. *She knows something. She just thinks she knows something. I wonder if she has talked to her grandmother. But Mrs. Medina doesn't know anything. I wish Lucy did know about the dolphins, but I promised them—I promised them I wouldn't tell.*

Chapter 12
Water Colors

The sky turned from black to gray to blue, but the sun had not yet shown itself. The sleepy-eyed girls stumbling out of the cabin and the seagulls squawking overhead woke the boys. Hugo walked out, climbed onto the dock, and spoke to the officials at the end of the pier. He came back and jumped down onto the yacht.

"Okay, kids, let's get this boat moving. We're going to have a great day."

"Where are we headed, Mr. Medina?" Will asked.

Hugo climbed up on the bridge. He leaned over the rail, "We'll go south to some little islands, the Exumas. I know where we can swim and snorkel and do some great fishing."

He went to the controls and the engines roared to life. After untying the lines, the dads jumped on board. The engines grew louder as the big boat moved away from the dock and out into the harbor.

Paul took some fishing line and tied a piece to each of the boys' hats. He tied the other end to a safety pin and then hooked the pin to the boys' shirts. "An old fisherman's trick; when your hat blows off, you won't lose it."

The boys nodded their approval. And, sure enough, before the boat had cleared the harbor, the wind blew their hats off, but none of them ended up in the ocean.

Will laughed as he put his hat on again, "We've got to tell everyone on the Key about this."

The men sat up on the bridge while the kids sat on the rear deck, watching the town of Nassau fade from view. The boat turned east out of the harbor and then south.

Hugo climbed down from the cockpit. Cruising south on calm waters, Jim and Paul now drove the boat. As Nassau disappeared, a string of islands came into view just off to the west. Some of these islands featured a palm tree or two, but no one lived there—other than the birds. Hundreds of gulls, pelicans, and sandpipers circled above.

Scattered throughout this part of the Bahamas, a few larger islands with sloping hills, dense trees, and a smattering of colorful buildings came into view. Hugo pointed to one of the islands.

"A hundred or so people might live on that island. Their boats and docks are on the other side in calm water, shielded from the winds coming from the open sea. They fish and relax and have a nice life." He turned and yelled up, "Jim, Paul, coffee?" The two men nodded.

Hugo went inside and came out with a thermos and three cups. He tossed the thermos up to Jim and then the cups, one at a time, before he climbed back up to the bridge.

They cruised for a while and then slowed down to do some fishing. The dads helped the kids put out their lines. After yesterday's adventure, the kids hoped to hook a sailfish. With his arms and legs still aching, Mike wandered around the boat, content just to watch the others.

The kids got a few bites and Clara caught a nice Spanish mackerel that the dads said would make a great dinner, but no one hooked the big one. As the sun beat down, the kids tired of sitting there doing nothing; so they pulled in their lines, and the girls gathered in the cabin to get lunch.

They couldn't believe it. The delicious leftovers from the day before were gone. Yesterday, they had put the remaining chicken and coleslaw back in the refrigerator. Now they stared at a plate containing a gnawed chicken leg and a few strands of cabbage.

"Way to go, guys," Diane said.

The boys gathered around the counter.

"What's the matter with you, Diane?" Rusty sneered at his sister.

"You ate everything. I can't believe it."

"It wasn't just me."

"Yeah," Bob said, "could be that the dads ate that stuff last night."

Lucy held up a plate with a few dark crumbs on it. "They ate all the brownies and the cookies."

The boys grinned.

"Thanks for saving some for us," Clara said. "What a bunch of little pigs!"

After a great show of indignation and name-calling, the boys gathered around the galley counter and began making peanut-butter-and-jelly sandwiches. With much pushing, reaching, talking, and laughing, the boys made the sandwiches for themselves, the girls, and they even delivered some up to the bridge for the dads.

After lunch, Hugo slowed the boat down and started moving toward two particular islands. The first island on the right had a long, white beach with plenty of palms. The land rose to a high plateau with a few brightly-colored houses on top. Other houses hung precariously on the side of the hill, their white tile roofs glistening in the sun. Little white footpaths twisted down the green incline, disappearing in the trees from time to time but reappearing and connecting the houses to the beach.

Hugo spoke up, "We're going through this channel. There's a bay with a sandy bottom and a reef on the other side. We can snorkel and swim there. It's a wonderful piece of the ocean."

"Dad has brought us here before," Lucy said. "It's a beautiful spot."

Bob chimed in, "Yeah, this is a great spot; there are more fish here than you've ever seen."

The *Las Olas* headed into the channel. Through the perfectly clear water, the shadow of the boat moved across the white sandy bottom.

The kids gathered at the back of the boat as they passed the two islands. On the island to the right, people stood on the beach, some waving at the yacht. To the left, hundreds of white gulls, brown pelicans, and other birds perched all over the rocks and hovered above them. The cries of the gulls filled the air. Occasionally, a cruising pelican would flap its wings as if putting on brakes, hang in the air for a moment, and then dive straight into the sea.

As the yacht passed through the channel, a long wooden pier came into view. The pilings of the pier stood a little crooked. Four wooden boats hugged the pier and many more sat up on the beach. Painted in bright island colors, each boat displayed a bold and unique pattern: red with yellow stripes, blue with red trim, green with polka dots of bright blue.

Mike sat on the rail at the back of the boat. He wondered if his dolphin friends came to these waters. The dolphins had told Mike that they traveled back and forth from Biscayne Bay to the Bahamas. Mike knew they considered every part of the sea their home, but he guessed "his dolphins" would particularly like this peaceful place.

Hugo climbed up the tower and drove the boat from the platform high above the *Las Olas*. From up there, he could see down into the water. The yacht now moved at a crawl. The children leaned over the side. The pink, purple, red, green, yellow, and orange of the reef beckoned to them as did the reef fish swimming in and out of the nooks and crannies of the coral.

Jim and Paul both stood at the bow, searching for a good place to drop the anchor so that the yacht would stay just off the reef.

Paul motioned to Hugo. "Right here, Hugo. The current will push us back toward the reef."

Hugo hit a button, and the anchor fell from the front of the boat. In a few minutes, the engines fell silent and the dads moved to the fishing deck, opened the door at the back of the boat, and unfolded the wooden platform that sat just touching the surface of the water.

Paul had blown up three canvas rafts. He tied them to the yacht with long ropes. If the kids got tired, they could hang on to those. They all had a mask, a snorkel, and flippers. Hugo gave instructions, "Now remember, don't touch the coral or grab anything. You could get stung."

The kids screamed and jumped in.

Rusty, Diane, Lucy, and Clara wore the yellow inflatable snorkeling vests that would just barely keep a swimmer afloat. They floated face down on top of the water and peered at the reef and the fish through their masks. Everyone tried to keep their heads in the water and use the snorkels to breathe. The snorkels proved to be a challenge, and now and then someone would breathe in a little seawater and come up coughing. Mike wondered if the dolphins ever breathed in any water and came up coughing. *Probably not,* he thought.

Bob and Mike swam around the reef with their masks and flippers. They dove down and swam over the coral, taking in the colorful sights. Hundreds of fish darted out and then back in to their little hiding places when the boys got close.

Skimming above the coral in front of Mike, Bob glided over the top of a smooth, round coral head and dove down the other side. Mike lost sight of his brother. Then he heard an underwater gurgling scream. Bubbles came up from the other side of the big coral followed by Bob, who shot to the surface. Mike came up as Bob gasped for air.

"Watch out, Mike! He's huge! I almost ran into him!"

"W-what?

"Over there, the deep water!"

Bob swam past Mike. Mike took a deep breath and went down. He swam to the round coral, peeked over the edge and gulped. The huge barracuda, now below him, had to be bigger than his brother. Built for speed with a pointed snout and a long lean body, Mike knew the glistening silver barracuda was known to attack its prey with lightning strikes—its long, razor-sharp, jagged teeth ensuring a kill every time.

Mike had been around plenty of barracuda before. Over at the marina, charter fishing boats would come in and throw them up on the dock. The charter captains always complained about the barracuda snapping up the fish their clients had on the line. With barracuda hanging around waiting for an easy meal, the tourist fishermen could never reel in a hooked fish fast enough. The captains of the Key disliked the barracuda; however, they respected the sleek fish as one of the great predators of the sea.

None of the barracudas brought in at the marina could ever match the size of the one now in front of Mike. It hovered in the water. Only its tail moved slowly back and forth.

Mike turned around on the surface. Will, Lucy, Clara, Diane, Rusty, and the three dads swam over. They floated on top and gazed down at the fish. Slowly, they turned and eased back to the rafts where Bob hung on, waiting for them. The kids laughed hysterically.

"W-way to g-go, B-Bob."

"Did you bump into him?" Will said, "I'll bet you pooped in your bathing suit."

Bob swung at his brother. "That's not funny, Will."

"Kids," Hugo said, "that barracuda won't bother you as long as you don't spook him. I don't want any of you to go back over there."

For hours, the kids floated, swam, bobbed up and down, and explored the reef. They would come together when someone made an unusual discovery. Every inch of the reef teemed with life.

Paul took a hunk of mottled, gooey ice the size of a gallon jug and put it in a bag made of fine fish net. The pink and brown block smelled of dead fish. "Get ready kids, I'm going to put out the chum."

The ice contained stale fish blood, little pieces of shrimp, and specks of guts from cleaned fish. Paul shook the bag in the water and as the ice melted, the bits of fish and blood began to float in the water.

The cloud of fish food floated over the reef, and hundreds of fish swarmed out of their sanctuaries in the coral. Black-and-white sergeant majors, queen angels, blue devils, banded coral shrimp, and parrotfish swam everywhere. Even an occasional sea horse drifted into view. Little flashes of color zipped and darted about eating the food. They resembled bits of multicolored confetti, fluttering in the water.

The children floated motionlessly, as some of the more curious fish came up and pecked at the glass in their masks. The sights, shapes, colors, and peculiar fish so amazed Mike that he didn't know where to turn first. He almost forgot to breathe.

As he floated, Mike thought about his dolphin friends. *I bet they like to zip around reefs like this. Where are they? Hey, Nyla, Naar, where are you? I wonder how far my thoughts can travel. I guess not very far.*

Chapter 13
The Storm

A line of dark clouds boiled up, and the wind started to blow a little harder than a tropical breeze. When the rain began, the snorkelers got back on the boat for a little rest.

"Those tropical fish were beautiful," Lucy said, "An angel fish came up and bumped against my swim mask."

"One ate a piece of food right out of my hand," Clara said.

Will said, "It was like swimming in the big fish tank in the lobby of the Beachside Hotel, only cooler."

"Hey, Bob," Diane asked, "were you just a *little* scared when you ran into that big barracuda?"

"Naw, he didn't bother me."

They all laughed. Smiling, Bob's face grew a little red.

The rain passed and Bob stood on the rail, "Let's go!" As he fell into the water he yelled, "Barracuda where are you!" The rest of them followed, screaming, "Barracuda!" as they jumped.

"Mr. Butler," Clara called out, "How about more fish food?"

Paul waved and soon the reef fish swarmed again in their frantic but gentle feeding frenzy.

Mike floated along, letting his arms and legs flop out next to him in the water. He could hear himself breathing through the snorkel in the quiet water.

Drifting with the current, he floated off the reef into deeper water, where the white sand bottom reflected the sunlight.

Hello, are you Mike? A voice came to Mike.

Mike jerked his head to the right. A dark dolphin with light gray and white stripes down his sides skimmed across the bottom. The big dolphin circled below him, came up for air, and then dove back down.

Yes, I'm Mike. Who are you?

I'm Riley. The dolphin slowed in front of Mike.

That's a different kind of name. Where did you get it?

I got it from my ancestors. It's a long story. I'll tell you someday, but not now. There's a big storm out at sea and it's coming this way. You need to go to a safe harbor soon. Tell your father and friends to get to land.

When will the storm be here?

We're not sure... tonight or tomorrow. The dolphin turned and raced back out toward the open sea. *Good luck, Mike.*

But where should we go?

Head for Nassau or some other safe harbor.

Mike lifted his head out of the water. He saw the dolphin burst out of the water in a low jump.

Swimming back to the yacht, Mike wondered how he could tell his dad the news of the coming storm. He knew he couldn't tell the men that he'd heard it from a dolphin.

Mike crawled up onto the platform. He took off his vest, flippers, mask, and snorkel and got a towel. The rest of the group still swam or floated over the reef. From the northeast, another bank of dark clouds moved over the island. It began to rain again. Hugo shouted, "Okay, kids, let's come in for a while."

The wind picked up as little waves lapped against the side of the boat and the kids dried off and changed clothes. The boys dozed on the couches in the main cabin, and the girls gathered downstairs.

The rain stopped as quickly as it had begun. The sun came out again, but the wind blew harder and steadier now. Unable to sleep, Mike sat on the rail at the back of the boat, pretending not to listen to the three men standing across from him, staring to the east and out to sea.

"That band of squalls," Jim pointed toward the dark clouds coming from the open ocean, "will be here in a half an hour or so. What do you think, Hugo?"

"Well, nothing has come over the radio, and this is a good, sheltered spot. We could just stay here until morning and then run back to the Key. You know, we just can't head that way," Hugo said as he motioned to the west, "there are no deep channels, just a bunch of reefs and shoals. We would run aground for sure. We'll have to go north and then cut back west toward Miami."

"Why don't we go north now?" Paul asked. "We could make it back to Nassau Harbor in about four hours. It would only be a little after dark."

Jim added, "Yeah, we could head north, and if we thought it would be easier, we could turn before Nassau and run west."

Hugo nodded. "Okay, let's get the boat ready. We'll head for Nassau right after this next storm band passes us."

Mike took a deep breath and, almost imperceptibly, nodded. His dad and the other men knew what to do. The men knew the signs, though none of them used the word *hurricane*.

The next band of wind and rain came in twenty minutes with more intensity. The wind swung the *Las Olas* around. The anchor chain strained to hold the boat in place. Below the surface, the anchor slipped along the sandy bottom. Nobody noticed the yacht drifting toward the reef.

The boat bobbed up and down as the waves began to grow. A crunching sound came from the back of the boat. Something thumped against the hull. Hugo came running up from below, with Paul right behind him. They burst out of the cabin and leaned over the side. Jim came from up front.

Paul pointed down. "We've drifted over the reef. The water is only two feet deep." The *Las Olas* banged down again against the coral.

"The anchor is slipping. We've got to go now." Hugo said as he climbed up the ladder to the bridge. The engines roared to life. The boat inched away from the reef as the winch began pulling up the anchor.

The roar of the engines and the grinding of the anchor winch woke everyone. The girls climbed up from below, and the kids now gathered in the main cabin. The rain poured down, becoming heavier by the minute.

Paul stumbled through the door.

"Anything wrong, Daddy?" his daughter asked.

"No, nothing, sweetie," he turned to the kids with a reassuring smile. "With all this rain, we decided to go back to Nassau."

"Do you think we can go shopping in Nassau again?" Clara asked.

"Sure," Paul said, "I don't see why not."

Bob stared out at the rain.

"When the rain stops," Bob said, "can we put out some lines? I want to try again for a fish like Mike's."

"We're going to be moving fast and it might be a little rough," Paul smiled, "But we might give it a try when the rain stops."

Paul opened the door. The rain beat down. "You kids stay inside." He slammed the door.

Mike sensed the seriousness of the coming storm and knew there would be no more fishing.

The three men gathered up top on the bridge, as the boat moved between the two islands and out into the open sea. The island to the south with the barren rocks appeared different. The waves crashed against the rocks and spewed white foam over them.

Bob pointed to the big rocks on the far island. "Where did the birds go?"

"Yeah that's weird," Lucy said.

"It sure has gotten windy," Will said in a quiet tone.

"Watch out!" Lucy tried to grab Clara as she lost her balance and tumbled across the cabin. "You okay, Clara?"

"I'm okay. It's getting rough out there," Clara said, as she rubbed her elbow and winced a little.

Diane pressed against the window. "I don't like this. These waves are huge."

Rusty stood next to her. "Don't worry, Diane, this is a big boat."

Diane's eyes darted back and forth nervously.

"It's not that big," Clara said.

With ever growing swells now rolling past the boat, no one wandered back outside. The wind sliced at the tops of the waves and turned the water into white spray that smacked against the windows. The little low islands to the west now became harder to make out. As the boat rose up on a wave, white surf outlined the islands, but when the boat dipped down, the islands disappeared. A black, foreboding sky loomed in the east, while in the west, the sky gleamed with shades of blue, pink, and gold as the sun set.

The door flew open and Paul and Jim, soaking wet, pulled themselves into the cabin. The wind whistled, and the engines roared.

"Kids, I want you all to put on life jackets," Jim said. No one objected as Jim opened the chest and tossed the vests on the floor.

"I'm not feeling so good," Will said, as he put on his life jacket.

"Let's go, kids. Get these on now," Jim said.

The children moved and Jim checked each of the vests, making sure they fit snugly. He smiled at each child but no one smiled back. Lucy and Diane took deep breaths with wide eyes as they tried to fight off the first feelings of sea sickness.

Hugo burst through the cabin door. "You got it, Paul?"

"Yeah!"

Hugo grabbed Jim and whispered something to him. Hugo ran up to the cockpit, joining Paul.

Jim said forcefully, "Kids, listen to me. Keep your life jackets on and stay inside."

"Is everything okay, Mr. Connelly?" Clara asked.

"Yes, Clara. We're just going to go through some rough seas," Jim patted Clara on the head. "We'll be back in Nassau in a while."

The children sat together on the floor.

"I think they're worried." Clara motioned toward the three men.

"My dad has sailed this boat in rough seas before," Lucy said.

"This is a big boat." Rusty said.

"You keep saying that," Diane snapped. "Shut up."

"What do you think, Bob?" Will asked.

"I think it's getting rougher," Bob said in almost a whisper.

"It's g-going to g-get a l-lot r-rougher." Mike got up and stumbled toward the cockpit.

"I don't know, Jim," Hugo said, "I can feel the vibration, and the starboard engine is working harder. If it's the prop, we might be able to use it. If it's the shaft, who knows? I've never run in seas this big. I don't know how fast we will be able to go." Mike could sense the tension in Mr. Medina's voice, and there was no mistaking the fear in the eyes of his dad and Mr. Butler.

Nyla, Naar, where are you? We may need your help. Can you hear me? Then Mike thought to himself. *Good thinking, Mike, how could they help us anyhow? Nyla, Naar, can you hear me?*

"I've got the wheel," Paul said as he stepped next to Hugo. "Go below and see if you can tell what's happened."

Feeling a little sea sick, Clara and Diane sat listlessly on the bed in the stateroom holding on to each other.

Mike followed the men to the engine room.

"Mike, stay behind me, it's too crowded down here," his dad said.

Hugo opened the small door to the engine room. The roar filled the boat. Mike watched at the door as the two men bent into the engine room, filled with wires and cables and the hot gunmetal engines. They had to crouch to move, and only one person could walk between the engines. With water sloshing around his feet, Hugo inched to the back. He peered over the engines and then worked his way out of the confined space. The men and Mike climbed back up to the cockpit. Paul struggled to keep control of the wheel.

The marine radio crackled. "Seas ten to twelve, winds out of the north-northeast, gusting to fifty knots."

Paul said, "Let's hope it doesn't get any worse."

Hugo worked at the controls. "I'm turning on the pumps. They should handle the water. There is a vibration; probably the propeller is bent and maybe the shaft. If the vibration gets too bad, we'll have to shut down the starboard engine."

The next squall line of fast-moving black clouds and howling winds hit them. The rain drove at the boat sideways, and visibility deteriorated to a few yards. The waves now rose up higher than the bow.

"These seas are getting higher than twelve," Hugo announced.

Jim and Paul grimaced, as the big boat slammed into the next giant oncoming wave. The sea crashed on top of the bow, and foaming water rolled back to the cockpit, as the windshield wipers flopped back and forth uselessly.

Hugo reached up and grabbed the throttles controlling the engines. "We've got to slow down." He pulled back on the two sticks a little. "We hit too many more like that last one, and we'll get swamped."

The three men gripped the dashboard. Hugo stared out the window. "It'll be dark soon. If we keep on this heading, we should be able to find the Nassau lighthouse off to the west. When we're north of the lighthouse, we can turn west and then into the harbor."

Paul and Jim nodded in agreement.

Hugo turned. "I'm going down to check out the engines again."

Hugo went down through the main cabin. The kids sat close together in a front corner. "Don't worry, kids. We'll be okay." The sounds of the howling wind, the waves crashing against the boat, and the roaring engines drowned out his words.

Boiling, churning seas surrounded the yacht, as complete darkness came sooner than the men expected. When the boat settled between two waves, the mountains of water swelled higher than the tower above the yacht. *Las Olas* rode up one side of a wave and then plunged down like a giant roller coaster. Fishing gear and tackle boxes rolled and tumbled inside the cabin. The kids frantically stuffed gear into the bins in the benches, but controlling the mess proved impossible.

Hugo came up from below and jumped up to the cockpit. Jim now stood at the wheel with Paul next to him.

Hugo asked, "How long since we left the channel down south?"

"About four hours." Paul said. "With seas like this and a damaged prop, we might only be halfway to Nassau."

Hugo grabbed the radio microphone. "There is more water in the engine room." He flipped the switch. "Mayday, mayday. This is *Las Olas*. We are south-southeast of Nassau. Mayday, mayday." The crackly sound of static, and nothing else, came from the radio.

Mike kept calling out to the dolphins but no thought waves came back to him.

Forcing smiles for the children below, the men put on their life jackets. The children huddled against the side of the cabin, their faces pale, and their eyes wide.

The yacht bounced, twisted, and rocked. *Las Olas* lurched to the left as a huge wave crashed into it and the windshield shattered into pieces. Broken glass and water inundated the dashboard and the instruments. Another window in the cabin burst. A deluge of seawater gushed into the main cabin as Lucy, Will, Bob and Rusty tumbled to the other side of the boat, screaming. Mike held on to the rail just behind the cockpit.

Paul shouted down, "Kids, move behind the counter in the galley or downstairs!"

Frozen with terror, no one moved.

The boat climbed another mountainous wave. The water in the cabin—along with the pillows, bottles, glasses, baskets, and boxes—sloshed to the back. The back door sprung open—the sea water and most of the now flotsam and jetsam flowed out onto the fishing deck. Lucy fell and slid toward the opening, arms and legs flailing about, too terrified to do anything but grunt. Gasping, Mike dove toward Lucy. Bob and Will got to her first, grabbed her, and pulled her to the side. The boat started down the wave, and the remaining loose objects throughout the boat swept forward.

Mike crawled toward the open cabin door. He struggled up at the doorway and stood on the outside step. As he reached for the door-knob, his foot slipped and he tumbled down, slamming against the teak planking. The wind whipped the door shut, and a wall of water crashed over the stern, throwing Mike hard against the side of the yacht. With the wind knocked out of him, his vision blurred, and blood pouring down his face, Mike pulled himself up. Slumped against the fighting chair, he felt himself fading toward unconsciousness, as another wave ripped him away and swept him into the blackness of the sea.

In the cockpit, Hugo and Paul gripped the wheel, fighting to hold the yacht against the assault of the hurricane. Jim worked with the radio again. "Mayday, mayday. Mayday. This is *Las Olas,* south-southeast of Nassau. Mayday, mayday."

The kids gathered in the front of the cabin and headed down the stairs, holding on to each other.

Water continued to pour through the window into the cabin. Bob and Rusty grabbed a cushion and stuffed it in the jagged broken window. Bob turned to Will. "Get Mike and find some more cushions!"

Will nodded. He turned around and found one immediately. He gave it to Bob. Lurching across the cabin, Will found another water-soaked cushion. Rusty took it. Will turned around and searched for Mike. He stumbled down the stairs where Lucy sat in a corner. "Where is Mike?" Will asked.

"He's not down here."

Fear began to overcome Will. Sensing something horrible, he jumped back up to the cabin and turned to the cockpit. Will screamed, "Dad, I can't find Mike!"

Puzzled, Jim came down into the cabin. "Mike!" he yelled out. Rusty and Bob held the cushions in the broken windows. Jim jumped down the stairs, "Lucy, where is Mike?"

Lucy stood, now worried. "I don't know, Mr. Connelly. I haven't seen him since—"

Not waiting for an answer, Jim squeezed past Lucy toward the stateroom. He sloshed through the water, moving from room to room, frantically pulling open the doors. He ran back up the stairs, his panic turning to terror. Paul stood in the cabin. Terrified, Jim grabbed Paul by the shoulders. "Mike is missing."

Jim pushed past Paul, ran to the back of the cabin, and flung the back door open. Jumping down on the back deck, Jim fell toward the fighting chair and clung to it.

Jim peered out at the roiling black sea through the driving rain. He screamed into the wind, "Mike! Mike!" A wave crashed over him.

From the cabin door, Paul shouted above the howling wind, "Jim, get back in here! Jim!"

Jim grabbed the railing and pulled himself back into the cabin.

The two men struggled up to the cockpit. Jim grabbed Hugo by his life vest. "Mike is missing."

Hugo turned to Jim in disbelief. "How?"

"I don't know. We've got to turn around. Come on, Hugo, Now!" Jim grabbed at the wheel and tried to turn it.

"Okay Jim, Okay. Let me handle her." Hugo tugged back on the wheel.

The kids gathered in the cabin. Bob's mouth fell open as tears rolled down his cheeks. Will sat next to him, his face in his hands. Rusty pushed his face against a window. The girls hugged each other. No one spoke. No one wanted to think about the nightmare now confronting them.

Hugo started to turn the wheel and then hesitated. "I don't know if we can turn, Jim."

"Hugo, for God's sake!" Jim's eyes filled with tears, his face contorted with fear, and he gripped Hugo's life vest even tighter. "We've got to find Mike!"

Hugo turned the wheel harder to the left. A huge wave caught *Las Olas* as she climbed the mountain of water, now at a precarious angle. The yacht's left side plunged underwater. Everyone hung on as the boat dipped. Hugo turned back to the right, "If I get her sideways and a wave catches us, we'll capsize."

Jim stumbled to the back of the boat and opened the cabin door. Through his tears, he stared out at the menacing sea. Turning back to help the others fight the storm, Jim silently said a prayer for Mike. He knew they faced a deadly challenge. He knew they couldn't risk losing the boat. He had to think of Bob, Will, and the others. Jim closed his eyes as a dull pain gripped his stomach. *Please, God help us.*

Chapter 14
The Great Secret

Unconscious, and with blood running across his face, Mike rode up and down the huge waves in his orange life jacket.

I've got him; he's just ahead, Pike said as he swam ahead of the others. Four big dolphins circled around as the waves threw Mike's limp body up and down.

The dolphins' echolocation skills made it easy for them to find Mike in the dark, turbulent sea.

Is he alive? Riley asked.

Yes, he's breathing, and I can feel his mind, Salvador said.

He can't stay in the water very long, Finn said.

I can get to a strap hanging from his vest and pull him, Salvador suggested.

Good, but don't pull him too fast or, he might drown. Finn and I will swim under him and keep him up, Riley added.

Salvador grabbed the strap. *Finn's right. We've got to get him out of the water soon. Let's take him to Darius' island. Pike, you go and tell the others.*

Pike shot away to the south.

They took turns supporting Mike, and pulling him up and down the monstrous waves.

They pulled Mike toward the island for hours, until they brought him to the place where Darius lived. Here, Mike would be sheltered from the wind and waves.

We think he is close to dying. His head is bleeding. You must help, Salvador said.

I will. I'm waiting for you. Hurry.

Mike's limp arms and legs bobbed in the water, as he floated on his back. The wind still howled in the night sky, but now with less ferocity.

The rain pelted down as Darius ran out in the water and scooped up Mike in his arms. "So, this is the brave shark fighter," he said aloud to himself, "I wonder how all that courage and spirit fit into this boy. Let's see what we can do to help you."

Darius, a lank, lean island fisherman, had strong dark arms and big rough hands. His bushy, black hair glistened like shiny little black wires.

Darius walked to the shore. He brought Mike to his hut and placed him on a cot. He stripped off Mike's life vest and wet clothes, covered him with blankets, and pressed a white cloth against the gash on his head.

Darius put oil lamps near the bed for warmth and began rubbing Mike's hands, arms, and legs. He told the dolphins what little he knew. *He is still unconscious. There may be nothing I can do.*

You must help him. Take him below to Krondal, said Salvador.

I can't do that.

Darius, this is a special boy. You must at least ask for permission to bring him to the ship.

Darius continued to try and revive Mike.

One Seventy-Three, A thought from far away came to Darius.

Yes, Sir, Darius said.

Bring the boy to the ship and take him to Doctor Verleor.

Yes, Sir.

Darius wrapped Mike in a blanket and held the limp body to his chest. Walking out into the darkness and the rain, he moved quickly through the palms behind his hut, until he reached a massive boulder. Darius stood next to the rock for a moment, and it slid silently to one side revealing a hole that resembled an old water well.

Clutching Mike in his arms, and with his mind holding at bay the force of gravity, Darius stepped out into the air and floated down to a sandy floor. He stared at the rock surface that surrounded him and a portion of it slid open. A long, silver tunnel, big enough to walk through, curved in front of him. Floating just a few inches above the floor, and with a faint glow of light following him, Darius moved down the pipe. At the end of the passageway, another pipe descended into blackness. Darius stepped out, pressed Mike's limp body to his chest, and shot down.

Do you think we saved him? Salvador asked.

Yes, he is in good hands now, said Riley.

Should we stay here? Finn asked, as the three dolphins circled in the sheltered lagoon of Darius' island.

Salvador swam near the rickety dock. *Let's stay for a while. I'm sure Nyla's pod and Pike will be here soon.*

That's a good idea, but I think one of us should follow that yacht, Riley said.

I'll go with you, Finn said. *If that boat sinks, those people will need help.*

Riley turned toward the open sea. *You're right, Finn, come on.*

Mike lay on a table. A white sheet covered him to his waist. Flickering bright lights and multicolored beams shot around the room. A beam of soft, green light fell on Mike's chest from a silver pod floating above. The pod hummed almost imperceptibly. Three other beings sat at consoles in the room. Dr. Verleor wore a long white gown and white gloves; she passed a shining silver wand back and forth over Mike. The doctor read the little screen on the scanner.

Krondal and Captain Altrain walked into the room. *How is young Mike?*

He'll be fine, Admiral. I have repaired his wounds and restored his body rhythms. He should be waking soon. He'll need some food. His stomach is empty.

We will prepare a meal.

Is it true about the dolphins? the doctor asked.

Krondal nodded. *Yes, they have all come.*

All of them?

Well, almost all of them—as many as could get here in a few hours—and a good number of the whales. Some are still on the way to the dome. We knew that someday we would choose another human contact. As before, the dolphins have chosen for us. I think they have chosen wisely. Krondal and Altrain walked to the door. *When he wakes, bring him to my quarters,* the admiral ordered.

I have a skwill standing by who has changed into an island woman. She will be the first person Mike encounters. I want to ease Mike into seeing us for the first time.

Krondal turned in the doorway. *You're right, Doctor. Please take your time. Let us know when Mike is ready to meet us.*

As Mike woke up, he saw someone standing near him.

"Hello, Mike. I am Halima."

Mike's vision cleared, and he saw a young woman wearing a plain green dress stepping toward him.

How does she know my name? Where am I? Mike's eyes sprung wide open.

"You're in a hospital, Mike. You're okay."

"Wh-what ha-happened?"

"The storm washed you overboard. The dolphins rescued you and brought you here."

Mike surveyed the room. *The dolphins?*

"Wh-where are my d-dad and b-b-brothers, m-my f-f-friends?"

"They're well, they're on the yacht heading for Nassau."

"Are y-you sure? H-how d-do y-y-you know? Wh-where is this p-place?"

Halima put her hand on his shoulder. "Mike, this hospital is operated by very special folks. You will meet them soon, and they will seem strange to you. Don't be afraid. They are kind and gentle."

A little nervous, Mike nodded his head as he rose up on one elbow. He thought she seemed nice, but he wondered about his clothes. Feeling a little flushed, Mike clutched the sheet.

Doctor Verleor walked back into the room. Mike jumped. He almost fell off the table as he sat up, breathing hard and wide-eyed. Mike watched the doctor as she moved closer to the table. Her long, thin female body stood taller than his dad and supported a head that Mike thought to be much too big. The doctor's skin, the color of dark brown mahogany, caused her head to resemble a misshapen, husked coconut with patches of short-cropped brown hair. Her tiny ears and mouth appeared even smaller next to her huge nose, like a camel's with big nostrils that twitched and flared. She wore a flowing white, long-sleeved robe that fell to the floor. A white belt cinched it at the waist.

A space man, some kind of space man. It can't be. The dolphins—the dolphins brought me here. They know about this place. Mike's thoughts flew around his head.

Halima put her hand back on Mike's shoulder. "It's okay, Mike, this is Dr. Verleor."

"Hello, Mike. Please don't be frightened. You are safe." The doctor slowly reached out and patted Mike on the foot with her big, six-fingered hand. Mike twitched. Her calm, measured voice possessed a reassuring, almost motherly tone. Yet the doctor's luminescent blue eyes, accented by a slight glow of light from behind the iris, had an eerie quality about them.

Mike's eyes darted around the room.

"How do you feel?"

"I-I'm f-fine, wh-where are m-my d-dad and b-brothers?" The nervousness caused Mike to stutter even more.

"They're heading for Nassau. The storm is subsiding, and they should be safe. We're going to get you back to them soon. Mike, you are in a ship, deep below the ocean. I want you to meet some other members of our crew. We will explain all of this to you. Please don't be frightened."

"Are y-you a M-Martian?"

"No, Mike, but I am from far away. We are known as 'Seegans'. Are you strong enough to get up?"

"Y-yes," Mike nodded. "I th-think so."

The doctor eased Mike off the table and wrapped him in a sheet. She helped him get dressed.

Mike stood in front of a mirrored panel. He had on a long, white robe with a white cord around his waist, and he wore white socks and white sandals.

Mike thought, *She said the dolphins brought me here. How? They wouldn't take me to a place where I might get hurt. Where are the dolphins now?*

The two walked out of the examining room and into a great hall, as wide as a four-lane highway. The ceiling towered fifty feet above them. A slight green glow radiated throughout the almost dark hallway. As they walked down the massive corridor, a bright light appeared in each section they entered and then disappeared behind them.

"This is a big ship, Mike," the doctor explained, "and we only light areas when it is necessary."

The size of the passageways and the creatures floating from place to place amazed Mike.

The doctor pointed up at the floating gangly beings. "Those are skwill. You might call them robots. They help us with many things, and you should know that these skwill have the ability to change their appearance. They must, however, keep their basic form and shape. For example, they could not change into a pelican, but they could change into a person like you, walking down any street, anywhere. Another reason we keep the ship dim is that the skwill possess perfect vision in the dark."

Mike's mouth gaped. He smiled at the wonder of it.

"There are four hundred skwill on board." The doctor pointed to a large nook in the hallway, where a dozen skwill stood leaning against each other, motionless, with their eyes closed. They wore identical silver jumpsuits from their necks to their ankles with three large, red symbols emblazoned across the chest. The skwill resembled the doctor, right down to their six-fingered hands.

"These skwill are just waiting to be activated and perform some job for us."

Mike and the doctor continued walking. A spot of light popped out of another corridor, turned, and started flying toward them. The doctor laughed. "The lightning bugs are out again."

The glowing, yellow lightning bug moved so fast that Mike could hardly keep his eye on it. The ball of light zipped high into the tangled pipes and conduits above, stopped, dove down, circled around, and flew right between the doctor and Mike. The insect slowed just long enough for Mike to see its body. *Wow—a huge lightning bug. You could light up the whole back yard with a jar full of these guys. You would need a very big jar.*

They came to a glass door bigger than the door at the fire station on the Key. It slid open silently. Mike could hear the sounds of birds as he walked into a green meadow. As far as he could see, trees, exotic palms, and flowering bushes grew. Birds flew overhead. Mike had never seen birds like these. A white egret, standing a foot taller than Mike, waded in shallow water. A solid red eagle flew overhead. Birds similar to blue jays, blackbirds, and seagulls soared above. The blue jays sparkled with the brightest blue feathers Mike could have ever imagined, the blackbirds' iridescent orange eyes glowed, and bright green feathers adorned the tips of the seagulls' wings.

A steel precipice loomed up around Mike as tall as the courthouse in Miami. Off in the distance, a waterfall tumbled from an opening and gently fell into a lake below.

"This, Mike," the doctor's hand swept across the panorama, "is the heart of our ship. You can't see it, but above us is a dome enclosing these various gardens that are bigger than the island you live on. We have traveled throughout the universe, gathering and learning. It is the purpose of our lives."

Overwhelmed, Mike couldn't comprehend and he couldn't speak.

The doctor pointed to a two-seat craft. When Mike sat down in the craft, belts moved across his waist and shoulders. The doctor sat down and picked up a silver wand the size of a fountain pen with tiny lights and buttons along its side. As the doctor pointed the wand, the craft silently rose up and slowly flew across the dome.

A bird, resembling an enormous hummingbird with a bright red head, a yellow chest, and a five-foot, droopy green tail, flew up next to Mike. The size of a Thanksgiving turkey, its wings made a buzzing sound, and Mike laughed out loud. Below, he saw trees, green fields, birds, and animals. For Mike, the scene resembled a bunch of strange animals roaming around a well manicured golf course.

"Wh-where are w-we g-going?"

"To see the Admiral," the doctor smiled, "Are you hungry, Mike?"

"Y-yes, I'm r-real h-hungry."

The hovercraft floated high up the sheer steel cliff and came to a garage sized door. It opened with a whoosh of air. "We'll just ride over to the Admiral's quarters."

Moving down another great corridor, the craft skimmed a few inches off the ground, and came to two shiny, gold doors. As the craft stopped, the seatbelts disengaged and the gold doors automatically opened.

Above a glossy white floor, clouds moved across a pale blue vaulted ceiling. Mike thought that the room could be as big as the auditorium at his school. Strange plants, bushes, and trees grew in huge, bathtub-sized terracotta pots that had been arranged around the room. Two Seegans stood near a big table at the far end of the room. Mike walked next to the doctor. The admiral and the captain wore beautiful uniforms: white pants with a light blue stripe down the side, and white shoes. Gold stripes and gold buttons adorned their sky blue coats. Mike thought they dressed in a much grander fashion than the policemen in Nassau or even anyone in the Orange Bowl Parade. The two creatures walked toward Mike. With their big brown hands and round fuzzy heads sticking out of their uniforms, Mike thought they resembled scarecrows—scarecrows dressed in fancy clothes.

The admiral smiled. "Hello, Mike. I'm Admiral Krondal, and this is Captain Altrain."

Mike shook the admiral's big brown hand.

"How are you feeling?"

"F-fine. A-a-am I on a f-flying s-saucer?"

The three Seegans smiled at each other. "Well, I guess you could say that," Captain Altrain grinned. The captain squatted down close to Mike. He put his hands on Mike's shoulders.

"You are safe, Mike. Don't be afraid."

Mike sensed that these creatures would not harm him and his nervousness began to subside. He worried about his dad, his brothers, and his friends, and what they must be thinking.

"We will get you back to your family soon," the captain said with a smile.

Just hearing those words made Mike relax.

The admiral walked over to the table. "Come over here, Mike, and have something to eat."

The table glowed with white light that came from a source inside the translucent table top. The four of them gathered together at one end. Beautifully displayed on the table sat steaming platters full of scrumptious, mouthwatering food: lobster, shrimp, french fries, coleslaw, and corn on the cob, in great mounds.

"Th-this l-looks g-great,"

A skwill came over and put down four cold bottles of Coke with straws sticking out.

"We like Coke," the admiral said, "Do you?"

Mike nodded and took a big swig.

The doctor picked up a plate. "What would you like, Mike?"

Mike pointed to the platters. "S-some sh-shrimp, and a l-lobster. C-can I h-have some f-fries?"

The doctor filled Mike's plate and put it in front of him. The other Seegans filled their plates. They sat down and began to eat.

"Wh-where a-are you f-from? Wh-why are you h-here?"

The admiral held up his hand. No sound came from his mouth. *Mike, use your mind to communicate with us.*

Mike's eyes widened. *You can talk to me like the dolphins?!*

The doctor sat next to Mike. She put her hand on Mike's arm. *Yes, we can communicate with our minds. And, yes, we taught the dolphins to speak—the same dolphins who now speak to you. Mike, you are the third human in four hundred and fifty earth years that has been able to talk to the dolphins with your mind. You are truly a special person.*

The admiral added, *Mike, the doctor is right. You possess a special gift. We have studied you, and we know you to be a thoughtful, quiet, smart young man. You are the third person on this planet to communicate with the dolphins, but you are the first human on earth to have visited this place. We let you see us and our ship because we trust you, and we want you to understand. We are here to protect the environment and this planet. We may need your help in the years to come. For now, you must keep our secret.*

I'll keep the secret, but how could I ever help you?

Not now, Mike. In the years to come, we'll be together again, and then you'll know.

Mike's brain exploded with questions. *Where are you from? How did you get here? Why did the dolphins pick me? Can I talk to the dolphins now?*

Mike, slow down and eat, Krondal said in a fatherly tone, *and then you can sleep for a while. When you are sleeping we will communicate with your mind and you will learn all you want to know. This will happen in a short time, and then we will take you to your family.*

I don't understand. How will you talk to me when I'm asleep?

We will come to you as a dream.

Mike wasn't sure what this meant, but he ate ravenously, mostly lobster. After dinner, he took a walk with the captain. The admiral and the doctor strolled a few steps behind them.

The group stopped in front of a door. Krondal faced Mike. *Good-bye, Mike. We will not contact you for a long time. But we will meet again.*

Captain Altrain took his turn. *Good-bye, Mike. You are a wonderful young man. We will be counting on you in the future.*

How? What do you want me to do?

We will contact you in the future.

Will you come to Key Biscayne?

Probably not. The dolphins will speak for us.

Mike nodded. *Thanks for helping me.*

Mike shook the Seegans' big brown hands.

The doctor accompanied Mike, as the two walked into a great room and toward a wooden, four-post bed, sitting there with no other furniture around it. Mike had never seen a bed this big. He and his brothers and Rocky and all of his friends could sleep in it.

In the darkness, the edges of the room were not visible and he could barely make out the hundreds of palms and tropical plants growing in the pots at the edge of the darkness.

Palms and other trees rustled in a gentle breeze as the bed glowed, lit only by the moon and stars sparkling in the ceiling.

He climbed into bed. The mattress fluffed around him like a cloud. The doctor pulled a blanket up over Mike, patted his head and smiled. The room grew darker as clouds drifted across the ceiling. Mike relaxed as the sweet smell of night-blooming jasmine, a smell that often wafted through his bedroom window at home, surrounded him. His eyelids grew heavy.

This is the wildest bedroom in the world.

Dr. Verleor's mental tone relaxed Mike. *Yes, I'm sure it is.*

Mike wanted to stay awake and think about every detail of this happening. He knew he would never go to sleep.

Mike watched as a globe of glass and steel began to float above the bed. Blue, yellow, and green light beams, as soft as silk ribbons, fell on him. Pinpoint dots of light danced on the covers, and Mike felt warm, as a perfect dream came alive.

As he slept, Admiral Krondal's thoughts came to Mike. *For millions of years, the Seegans have protected a law that respects the environments and lives of all the creatures of the universe.*

Some Seegans believed that our sacred law did not apply to them when they wandered far away from our home planet. Those renegade Seegans intended to plunder the environments of other planets. We followed them, and after a time our two great ships fought each other.

We damaged the other ship's propulsion system, and those Seegans sought refuge on planet Earth. Our ship sustained damage as well and we landed here to protect this beautiful and unique planet from them.

At this time, the two ships are buried under the ocean floor. Our ship is below the Bahamas. The other ship is north of the Bahamas, in a much deeper part of the ocean in the direction of Bermuda. The dolphins call them the "under Seegans". We taught many dolphins and whales how to communicate with us and mankind. They have helped us monitor the seas and watch the under Seegans.

We have remained here and watched the under Seegans and the development of humanity for four hundred and fifty of your years. The under Seegans are not able to move or attack us, nor would we attack them. Should such a battle take place, Earth would be destroyed. But remember, Mike, this impasse will end. Also remember that the under Seegans would take advantage of Earth if they could. Be careful, they are watching.

In his dream, Mike toured the ship. The endless, grand hallways circled inside the great steel disk, a disk of extreme proportions. The great dome in the middle rose high above the floor of the botanical gardens.

Mike marveled at the library. Two rows of white columns flanked the main reading room of the grand library. The size and beauty of the massive room defied the senses as the far end vanished in the distance. The black floor sparkled with lights representing constellations. Murals, depicting scenes from planets light-years away, spun across the vaulted ceiling. Millions of books filled the lavish, dark, wooden shelves radiating from the main room.

Skwill floated above, retrieving any source of information the Seegans requested. Silver discs hovered in the air. Beams of light shot out of them, directed at anyone reading. Mike saw dining rooms, a gym packed with strange equipment and gizmos, laboratories, observatories, and the control room where the Seegans directed and flew the ship. The semicircular room resembled an amphitheater. Tiers of seats cascaded down to an empty floor. Each seat had a television-like screen with a flattened typewriter in front of it, where the skwill and Seegans worked. The seats faced a screen as big as one at a drive-in theater, which displayed a mind-boggling series of numbers and images. A silver railing about four feet high stood above the uppermost row of seats. From behind the railing the Seegans watched and directed those below who operated the ship.

Mike stirred in his dream when he saw the great dome. To the west of the Bahamas, in deep water, lay an expanse of flat sand. When the Seegans wished, the sand parted, and a huge glass dome rose from the sea floor. The dome always stayed below the surface of the sea. The Seegans had built a vast labyrinth of tubular passages below the islands of the Bahamas, and they used one of these passages to visit the dome. Dolphins entered the dome through special openings at the base, and the pool in the middle of the dome usually teemed with dolphins. Seegans, wearing white shorts, swam in the pool. Their long bodies and big hands and feet made them excellent swimmers, and they loved to laugh and play with the dolphins. The dome represented a special place for the Seegans and the dolphins. At this dome, dolphins came to receive the power to communicate with their minds.

Krondal's voice came back to Mike. *Here, Mike, at the dome, is where we have enhanced the power of the dolphins' brains over the centuries. We have taught them many human languages and much of humanity's accumulated knowledge. We have, however, never been able to impart to the dolphins an understanding of man's personalities, characters, or his attitudes about himself or his fellow man.*

Mike, I want you to know about a most unusual thing that happened at the dome after you fell into the sea. Hundreds of dolphins—and even some of the whales—came to the dome to make sure you would be saved. These sea creatures demonstrated to us how they feel about you. They consider you to be one of them, and they have great respect for you.

Just remember, you must keep what you have experienced and heard a secret. When the time is right, we will ask you to help us reveal ourselves to your world. Trust in the dolphins and be careful.

Mike, one other thing: when you return to your world you will have changed. It is our gift to you.

Mike's mind spun. *This is not a dream. I must keep the secret. It will be hard. What change? What should I do? Where are the dolphins? When will the Seegans reveal themselves? That's going to be a great day. I sure would like to bring one of them to school with me. I wonder if the under Seegans will be watching me?*

Chapter 15
Darius

The sky grew lighter. To the west, almost below the horizon, the lighthouse at Nassau came into view. Jim saw it first with his binoculars. "There, Hugo, there it is."

Not another word was spoken as Hugo turned the yacht toward the island. Tears seeped from Jim's red eyes. He fought not to cry. He didn't want his boys to see him like that. An hour later, a battered *Las Olas* limped into the harbor. The children stood on the rear deck. Nassau had survived Hurricane Albert's fury with only minor damage. Roof tiles, shutters, and canvas awnings littered the streets.

Las Olas resembled a floating junkyard. The aluminum tower that once stood above the boat hung over the side, mangled by the storm. As the boat rocked, the twisted metal dipped in the water. Only a few tattered pieces of canvas survived and the teak fishing chairs now consisted of battered scraps of wood hanging around steel posts bolted to the deck. Cushions from the couches hung out of the broken windows.

Listing, the yacht floated up to the moorings. Jim frantically jumped up on the dock before the yacht stopped moving. He ran toward the police hut at the end of the pier.

The boys helped tie up the boat. Crying quietly, Will sat against one of the pilings.

Bob sat next to his brother. "Will, he's okay; he had on his life vest and we had to be real close to shore. I know he must have been thrown up on one of those islands."

Will pulled up his knees and put his head down.

Ashen-faced and red-eyed, the girls milled around the pier. A doleful cloud hung over the grim-faced and battered passengers of *Las Olas*.

An hour later, Paul and Hugo walked down the dock. Jim came back toward the yacht and the three fathers exchanged glances. They stood for a moment, each of them with the same sickened gaze. Jim broke the awkward silence in a low, almost distant tone.

"The Bahamians are sending out a search boat. The Coast Guard has three cutters coming from Miami, one to search for Mike and two to take anyone who needs medical attention back to Miami. There is no phone service, but some officials have contacted the mainland by radio. The Coast Guard will have someone get in touch with our wives and Clara's folks." Jim's voice cracked a little. "And Alice will know…"

Jim began to sob. He knew how desperate Alice would be and he wouldn't be there. Paul and Hugo both put a hand on Jim's shoulders. No one said anything. Jim silently prayed for Mike.

Will walked over to the three men and asked, "Dad, do you think Mike is okay?"

"Yeah, Will. We just have to find him."

"How long could Mike stay in the water?"

"I don't know, Will, but the water here is warm."

"What about sharks?"

Jim squatted down and held his son's shoulders. "Like I said, Son, I'm sure Mike is okay." Jim tried to express the confidence he did not feel. He didn't want to acknowledge any other possibility.

Will gave his dad a blank stare.

A wiry lean man walked at a brisk pace down the dock toward *Las Olas*. He had on white shorts, a white shirt with colorful ribbons pinned on the left side, white shoes with white kneesocks, and a white hat with gold braiding. "Mr. Connelly, please?" the naval officer called down.

"I'm Jim Connelly."

"I'm Captain James Fletcher of Her Majesty's Frigate, *Glorious*," he said with a markedly British accent as he pointed to the dark warship sitting at the end of the harbor.

"The police told me you'd be over. Thanks." Jim jumped up on the dock.

"I have two boys of my own, and I can only imagine how you feel. We are preparing to get under way, and we will do our best to find the lad." The captain gave Jim a reassuring smile and patted him on the shoulder, "I need to know where you think he went overboard."

Jim turned back to the boat. "Hey, Hugo, bring your charts over here." He pointed at the captain in white. Hugo and Paul brought out the charts and joined the other two men. They spread the charts out on a chest on the dock. Hugo showed the captain where they had been and the path they had taken to make it back to Nassau.

The captain rolled up one of the charts and shook everyone's hand.

"Captain, I'd like to go with you," Jim said.

"Of course, Mr. Connelly, but I have been told that an American Coast Guard cutter is already searching and that the Bahamians have enlisted the help of four or five boats. It would be better for you to stay here, considering that one of them may find your boy."

"You're right, Captain," Jim nodded.

"Mr. Connelly, we'll do all we can. We'll keep you posted by radio up at the Government House. I must be off." The captain turned and headed back toward his ship.

Men in white moved about, outlined against the dark gray steel of the ship. Jim said another silent prayer for his lost son as he stood on the dock and watched the British warship pass. The children remained quiet.

Strange, but recognizable smells came to Mike. He opened his eyes but didn't move as he realized that he now wore the tee shirt and shorts he had on when he was washed overboard. He squirmed a little and stared up at dark wooden beams and a tin roof. A man with bushy black hair and black eyes walked over to him and bent down close to his face. His eyes twinkled like pieces of shiny black marble and his sparkling white teeth jumped out against his dark skin. The stranger stood up and put his hands on his hips.

"Hello, young man. How do you feel?"

Mike sat up on one elbow. His orange life vest lay next to the cot. "I'm okay, who are you—where are we?"

"I'm Darius, and you are on one of the Exuma Cays. I call this one Darius Cay. Ha-ha-ha-ha! So what happened to you? Did you fall off a boat?"

"Yep, in the storm."

"Well, you know you almost drowned, but I think you're just fine now. I guess your folks will be searching for you. The sun will be up in an hour or so, and then I'll take you over to Nassau town in my boat."

"Thanks, Mr. Darius."

"No, just Darius, young man, and who might you be?"

"I'm Mike Connelly from Key Biscayne. Have you heard anything about a yacht named *Las Olas*? My dad, brothers, and friends are on it. We got caught in the storm."

"I haven't heard anything. But then I wouldn't out here. They probably made it to Nassau. I understand the storm did turn north late the other night."

Mike's mind raced, he knew he had not been dreaming. All that had happened: the hurricane, the space ship, the Seegans, had to be real. This strange island man had to be one of them.

"Darius, can we go to Nassau now?"

"No. We could easily run aground in the dark. Don't worry I'll get you there in a big hurry. We'll go as soon as there is a little light."

Two gas lanterns hung from the dark beams above. Lines of conch shells and sponges hung around the room. On the far side of the single room hung the gaping jawbone of a shark, its triangular jagged teeth pointing out. Mike shivered inside. Fishing nets and colorful cork buoys dangled from the rafters and between the beams. Cane poles leaned in every corner. Haphazard piles of lobster traps and wooden baskets spilled out in front of the hut. As Darius walked around the room, his head constantly bumped into things.

"How did you find me?"

"Well, young Mike, I was on the beach after the storm and I saw you near the shore. I ran out in the surf and just plucked you out of the sea and brought you to my house."

Mike squinted back at Darius, his lips pursed. *That is not even close to what happened.* He took a deep breath, "Yeah—well, thanks."

The smells of dried seaweed, salt water, and fish permeated the hut. A much more delightful aroma came from a big black iron pot cooking on an old wood-burning stove. The steaming pot smelled of lobster, onion, and tomato. Mike also detected the aromas of curry, pepper, and hot sauce; those smells sometimes came from his own kitchen, but here other strange and delightful odors filled the air. Darius saw Mike staring at the pot.

"Ah, that is Darius' famous seafood stew. It has lobster, conch, and crab in it. It's powerfully good. My friends come from all over these islands to get some." Darius got a metal bowl and dipped a ladle into the pot. "Here, Mike, try some."

Mike spun out of bed. The sanded, wooden plank floor felt smooth to his bare feet. He took the bowl and a spoon.

"Thanks."

The stew tasted warm and spicy—a little unusual for breakfast, but good just the same. Mike wished his brothers could be with him in this place. Darius' hut amazed Mike almost as much as the spaceship. A painting hung near the stove; it featured the same vivid colors as the paintings in the shop back in Nassau. It reminded Mike of his painting of the dolphins, and he wondered what had happened to it. He ate a little more of Darius' stew.

Then Mike saw it. *The same lump,* Mike thought. *Darius has the same lump on his hand as Wilson Crain. The sixth finger—they're hiding their sixth finger.* Mike almost broke out in a laugh.

Mike reached out with his mind, as he knew Darius had to be one of "them". *Darius, are you a skwill? How do you get to the spaceship from here? Can you contact the doctor and the admiral?*

Not acknowledging Mike's thoughts, Darius worked around his cabin.

Come on Darius talk to me—talk to me with your mind.

Mike watched closely but nothing happened. "How long have you lived here?"

"Most all of my life."

"Who else lives on this island?"

"Nobody, I have the island to myself."

"That's pretty lonely, huh?"

"Oh no, my friends come and visit all the time. I think they come mostly to eat my stew, but that's okay." Darius smiled a big island smile.

"Yeah," Mike grinned, "this is great." Mike's eyes widened, he gasped and looked down at the bowl, and his trembling hands. *I'm not stuttering. I haven't stuttered since I woke up.* His eyes became glassy. *What has happened to me? The doctor—the doctor said there would be a change. She fixed me. I can talk without stuttering. It's true—everything is true.*

Mike caught a twinkle in Darius' eye and a slight smile as the dark fisherman walked outside. Mike stood in the doorway wanting to scream and leap in the air but he held the joy inside of him, as he had always done. The hut stood a few feet from the beach, the water, and a short pier. A long, white, open boat floated at the end of the dock. A bit more modern than most of the boats Mike had seen in the Bahamas, this one lacked the island flair for color. The sky lightened and Darius began to gather a few things. "Well, Mike, it's time to go. We can head for Nassau now. Go and get your life vest."

Mike helped Darius load some water and a few supplies onto the boat.

"It's going to be a beautiful day," Mike said.

"The day is always beautiful on Darius island."

Darius walked toward the hut. "Just a few more things, I'll be right back."

Mike stood on the dock, *Nyla, Naar, are you out there?*

Hi, Mike, I'm Riley. Nyla and Naar aren't here right now.

Hello, Mike. It's Salvador. We're glad you're okay.

Hi, Riley, you're the one who warned me about the storm.

Yep.

And Salvador, you're the dolphin who helped me with the sailfish.

That's me.

Are you from around here?

We're spotted dolphins and we live out at sea most of the time. We followed your boat during the storm, and with the help of a few others, we pulled you here to Darius.

Gee, thanks. You saved my life.

You're one of us, Mike, Salvador said.

Is Darius one of them?

Yes, he is. Remember, Mike, He will never admit he is a skwill, and you can never tell anyone about him.

I understand. He's just like Mr. Crain.

Who is Mr. Crain? Riley asked.

Wilson Crain, the artist in Nassau, he gave me a painting and he has lumps on his hands just like Darius.

We know of no skwill located in Nassau, Salvador said. *He could be a skwill from the under Seegans. We will ask the Teachers. Be careful, Mike.*

Mike nodded.

Darius walked back up the pier with a canvas tote bag. "Let's be on our way."

The dolphins submerged and moved away.

The two started out. As the sun rose, Darius' boat skimmed across the flat water.

"How long will it take us to get to Nassau?"

"Oh not too long, we'll be there by late morning," Darius replied.

Mike sat next to Darius. "Did you hide somewhere during the storm?"

"Oh no, I stayed right in my little house. The island sheltered me."

Mike wanted to ask Darius so many questions.

Darius pointed. "Over there is a place where there is more conch than you could ever pick up."

The boat zipped along on the flat waters between the little islands. "Over there, between those two islands, is a reef with grouper around it the size of you."

They both laughed big belly laughs and Mike smiled at Darius. "Darius, are there many dolphins around here?"

"Oh yes, hundreds of them—hundreds. Mike, see that cay over there? Just behind it is some deep water with thousands of yellow tails and red snapper swimming about."

"I wish I could remember these places."

"Oh, you'll find them again someday."

Mike thought, *I wonder if it will last? It has to last. I'll be able to talk to people normally. What's everybody going to think? I'll be able to talk to Lucy. That'll be great.*

"How much longer to Nassau?"

"Over there." Darius pointed at the land now just visible on the edge of the horizon. "That's New Providence Island. Nassau is on the other side. We should be there soon."

"I hope my dad is there."

"I'm sure he will be."

Darius motioned off to the right. "You asked about dolphins. There they are."

Mike spun around. Twenty or thirty dolphins skimmed in and out of the water in perfect unison and now caught up to the speeding boat.

Hello, Mike. How are you?

Nyla, is that you?

Yes, and our pod and some others.

Hello, Mike!

Hi, Mike!

Mike recognized Naarin's mind. *Hey, Mike. You okay?*

Hi, Naarin. Yeah, I'm fine.

We knew you were in the best place you could possibly be. And now you know the great secret. It's an honor, Nyla said.

Naar told him the most important news. *Some of us followed your family and friends through the storm. They're safe.*

Thanks, that's great! Thanks for everything.

Farin described what he saw. *I went over to Nassau Harbor with Eshu and Risa. The people on the* Las Olas *went back to Miami on a Coast Guard ship. We think your dad is still in Nassau.*

Why didn't they go back on the Las Olas?

The storm hammered that boat. The only way it will make it back to Miami is on the back of a whale.

That would be a sight to see. Hey, I'm not stuttering anymore. The Seegans fixed my stuttering.

Yes we know, Nyla said.

Please tell them thank you for me.

We will, said Nyla. *We most surely will.*

Mike, we won't go into the harbor. It's too crowded right now. Good luck, Naar said.

We'll see you back in the inlet or at the cove, said Nyla.

Naarin piped up, *Hey, Mike, when you get back, we could go shark hunting.*

Let's hope you never get that close to a shark again. My nose still hurts from ramming that guy, Malak said.

Just kidding, Uncle Malak, just kidding.

The dolphins slowed down, fell back and disappeared. Darius gave Mike a smile and a slight nod.

The little boat sped into Nassau Harbor. Darius pulled up to the dock that ran along the main street. Darius stood up and reached his hand out for Mike. "Let's go."

Darius hoisted Mike up on the dock. A policeman, standing a few feet away, stared at Mike, who still wore his orange life vest. The policeman walked toward him.

"Hello!" Darius yelled from his boat below. "I got you young Mike Connelly here. The best catch I ever made."

The policeman's eyes popped wide open. "Are you Mike Connelly?"

"Yeah."

"The boy who was lost out at sea?"

"Yep, that's me. Do you know if my dad is here?"

"Oh my god," he said. He pulled a shiny silver whistle on a chain out of his top pocket. A high-pitched *tweet-tweet* filled the air. Two other policemen ran up.

The first policeman gripped Mike's shoulder. "This is the Connelly boy." Mike ran to keep up as the policemen hurried him down the dock to a tiny wooden shed with the word "Police" painted in red above the door. As they crowded through the door, they all began speaking.

"We got young Mike Connelly here," one of them said.

The policeman behind the desk grabbed the phone. "Are you Mike Connelly?"

"Yes, Sir. Is my dad here? Do you know where my dad is?" Mike began to worry. *What if the dolphins were wrong? What if my dad isn't here?* Mike sat on a wooden bench and fidgeted and his stomach churned. He fought hard not to cry.

The policeman dialed a number. "You won't believe this. The missing boy just walked into the station down at the dock.

"Yes. Mike Connelly. Down at the dock.

"Yes, yes. I think he is just fine to me.

"One of the patrolmen just walked him right in the door.

"I don't know.

"Tell his father to come straightaway."

The policeman grinned at Mike. "Well my boy, look out the window there—up the hill to the Government House."

Mike stood at the window and gulped, *Where is he?* Then Mike saw his dad running down the hill. He burst out the door and started running toward his dad. Tears poured down Mike's face. Jim scooped up his son.

"Oh thank God! Mike, Mike, are you all right?"

"I'm fine, Dad."

Jim kissed his son. He hugged him so hard Mike thought he wouldn't be able to breathe. They both cried and Mike buried his face against his dad's chest. His father's warmth and strong arms around him calmed Mike.

The policemen stood around them smiling. Mike noticed a man dressed in cotton pants and a tee shirt stained with bright, colorful blotches of paint. He stood down a side street in a doorway. Expressionless, the man turned and walked away. *Wilson Crain,* Mike thought. *He must have known that I would be here, but why is he here?*

Jim asked, "Who found him?"

"An island fisherman," the policemen pointed. "He's right over there in his boat."

They hurried down the dock. The boat and the fisherman were gone.

"Who was he?" Jim asked.

One of the policemen shrugged. "Well, in the excitement, I guess we didn't get his name."

Mike spoke out, "His name is Darius. He lives down on one of the Exuma Cays. He says the island is called Darius Cay."

The policemen laughed. "We'll find him, Mr. Connelly, and give him a proper thanks for you. Don't worry." The police sergeant said.

Mike walked with his dad. "Is everybody else okay, Dad?"

"Yep, they are all fine, thank God. They went back to Miami yesterday afternoon on a Coast Guard cutter. I stayed here to search for you."

Jim took Mike up to the Government House and thanked the smiling staff gathered on the front porch. A government official asked Mike and his dad to sit in his office. "So, Mike, tell me what happened to you."

"Well—I tried to shut the cabin door on the boat. I slipped and fell outside and I guess I hit my head. I got washed overboard and I woke up in a hut with a man named Darius. He brought me back here."

The man nodded. "Well, young man, you are very lucky."

Mike noticed his father staring at him in disbelief.

"Yes, he is lucky. Will you get a radio message to Miami as soon as you can? I need to let my wife know that we've found Mike and that he's safe."

"Of course, Mr. Connelly," the man said, "we'll do it right now."

Jim and Mike both shook the official's hand and walked down the hill toward the harbor.

"We're going back to Miami on a Coast Guard cutter. It should be in the harbor soon."

Mike smiled up at his dad.

Jim stopped and knelt facing his son. Mike saw the glaze in his eyes.

"Mike you're not stuttering anymore?"

"I know, Dad. I got knocked out in the storm and when I woke up I wasn't stuttering anymore." Mike shrugged and grinned.

Jim stood up and rubbed Mike's head. "That's wonderful, Mike."

It's way more wonderful than you think. I wish I could tell you.

"You okay, Mike?"

"Yeah, Dad, I'm fine. I just want to go home."

Chapter 16

Homecoming

Mike and his dad rode back to Miami on the sleek white ship. The captain let Mike sit in his chair on the bridge, as Mike chattered away about his adventure, never stumbling on a word. The cutter docked in Miami, with Mike and his dad standing at the railing, waving to Alice, Bob, and Will. The ramp touched down on the dock and the crew of the Coast Guard cutter clapped and cheered, as Mike flew down and ran into his mother's arms. Jim followed and hugged Alice and the boys.

"Jim, it's a miracle," she said.

"It's a miracle in more ways than one," Jim said, giving her another hug.

Jim and Alice sat in the front seat of the family car, and the three boys climbed into the back.

"Mike, what happened? How did you fall off?" Will asked.

"When I went back to shut the door, I slipped and a wave washed me over the side. I guess I hit my head, but I don't remember much."

Alice turned to the back seat and Mike caught her wide eyed expression of utter disbelief. She turned back to Jim. "How?" She asked in a low whisper.

Jim shrugged, "I don't know."

"Were you scared?" asked Bob.

"Nah, at least I wasn't as scared as you when you bumped into the side of that barracuda."

Will and Mike laughed. Bob punched Mike in the arm.

"Ow!" Mike elbowed Bob.

"Hey, Mike, you're not stuttering," Will said.

Mike shrugged his shoulders. As his eyes glistened and sparkled, he broke into a big smile.

The three boys talked and squirmed all the way back to the Key. When the family arrived back on the island, they pulled into the drugstore's parking lot. As the Connellys got out of the car, Rosa, Joan, and a group of neighbors hurried toward them. The group shared hugs, kisses, handshakes, and slaps on the back as they tried to speak at once.

"Mike, how are you?"

"Hey, Mike, where did you wash up?"

"Were you scared?"

"Who found you?"

Mike told his tale again: the wave, the island, the fisherman. Mike thought. *If I could tell them the real story. Now that would be something.*

Joan and Rosa realized the change in Mike. Their expressions of surprise spoke for them. No one said anything right away.

Bob sat on a stool at the counter. He unabashedly said it first. "Hey everyone, did you notice Mike isn't stuttering anymore?"

The little group of friends and neighbors stopped talking. Some of them cheered and patted Mike on the head. Joan and Rosa hugged and kissed Mike. Rosa made ice cream floats. On the counter, she lined up the cone-shaped glasses filled with dark, cold Coke and mounds of vanilla ice cream. The boys and the adults dug in. Rosa gave Mike a little wink.

Mike and his brothers chattered away with the rest of the neighbors.

Bob said, "The sailfish Mike caught—it had to be eight feet long."

"No, he wasn't," Will said, "but that barracuda that scared you was pretty big."

"I wasn't scared."

"Yeah, sure," Will snickered.

Bob sneered at him, as Will dug a spoonful of creamy white ice cream out of the dark liquid. "This is good stuff."

Mike concentrated on his glass. "I like the foam the best."

The neighborhood gathering dissipated and the Connelly family went home. Alice walked into the kitchen, as Mike stood in front of the open refrigerator.

Alice hugged him. "Are you okay, big guy?"

"Yeah, Mom, I'm fine."

"Do you want something?"

"No, just looking."

Mike walked out back to the dock. He thought about thanking his friends. He also thought about what he had learned from the Seegans. He wondered about those other two people who could communicate with the dolphins? What had happened to them?

Soon his dad and brothers appeared.

"School starts in two weeks, guys," his dad said.

"Yeah," Bob said. "Eighth grade is going to be great."

"Mike, why do you think you stopped stuttering?"

"I don't know, Will, but I don't feel any different—my tongue just works better now."

But Mike thought he would probably feel a lot different when school started.

Alice called from the kitchen, "Come on, boys. Dinner is almost ready."

The family came in and sat at the table. Alice handed Jim a glass. "A little toddy for you, dear."

"Thanks, Honey."

Alice stood by the dining room table. "Well, boys, tonight we're having lobster, potatoes, coleslaw, and key lime pie, all in Mike's honor. The lobsters are the ones Mrs. Medina brought over. I froze them, and I planned to cook them for a special occasion. This is certainly the night."

Returning from the kitchen, Alice carried the platter of split lobster tails with the white meat bulging out of the red shells. She then set down a bowl of boiled potatoes and a bowl of coleslaw.

Jim put two lobster tails on each plate. "Wow, guys, it doesn't get any better than this."

Alice served the potatoes and coleslaw. The table fell silent as they dug into the feast. Mike felt that he had been eating a lot of lobster lately. The homemade key lime pie topped off a perfect meal. As his family feasted on the delicious dinner, Mike talked at the dinner table in a comfortable and clear manner for the first time in his life.

"I wonder what happened to that sailfish," Mike said.

"Well, he is out there swimming around," Jim said. "Maybe another fisherman will hook him and have an exciting fight just like you did."

"Yeah," Will said, "and if the next guy lets that big sailfish go, he could be fighting for years."

Mike nodded.

Bob started to laugh, "You know, I just thought of something. Mike's going to win the prize at school this year."

They all stopped eating.

"You know, when Mike writes his essay about what he did this summer."

The table burst into laughter.

After dinner, everyone watched *The Ed Sullivan Show*. Bob fell asleep on the floor. Now too big to carry, his dad helped him into bed. Will and Mike staggered into their room. After crawling up on the top bunk, Mike lay in bed and stared at the painting of the dolphins Mr. Crain had given him in Nassau. His dad walked into the room.

"I found it in one of the chests on the yacht after the storm. Funny, it never got wet. I sent it home with Paul, and your mom hung it up here so you'd have it when you got home."

Mike smiled.

"Good night, Will; good night Mike." Their dad walked out and gently closed the door.

Will's voice came from below. "You sure were lucky, Mike. I'm glad you're home."

"Thanks Will. I'm glad you guys are okay too."

Mike continued to wonder—how could he help the Seegans reveal themselves to the world? He knew the Seegans had cured his stuttering, and he knew they understood how happy that would make him. Mike would keep the secret. He owed that to the Seegans. He owed that to the dolphins. He had made a promise and that was what mattered most.

Will, Bob, and Mike enjoyed the last days of summer, and every morning and evening, Mike stood on his dock hoping his friends would come.

A few days passed, and as the sun set over the bay, Mike saw three dolphins coming up the inlet. He knew they must be Nyla, Naar and Naarin.

Hi, Mike, they chorused.

Hi.

How are you feeling? Nyla's tone was concerned and motherly.

I'm fine. The Seegans told me that you saved me and that you asked them to help.

Some of our cousins saved you, Naar said.

And we did ask the teachers to help, Nyla added.

Thanks for being my friends. You saved my life.

Nyla became serious. *You are the only human to have ever met the Seegans. Mike, you now have the knowledge that our kind has had for hundreds of years.*

But why me?

You were born with a special power, and time will tell why the Seegans revealed themselves to you.

"Mike!" Alice called from the kitchen. "It's time for dinner."

I have to go now.

Nyla smiled, *We'll see you soon. Come to the cove when you have time.*

Bring a book to read to us. Naarin bounced a little in the water.

Son, Mike can't read to us all the time.

It's okay. I love reading.

"Let's go, Mike!" his mom called.

I've got to go, see you tomorrow.

Good-bye Mike, the dolphins turned and swam toward the bay.

Mike walked to the house. *I better talk to them about Lucy. She's catching on—no way, she can't know. If I say something to Nyla she might think I told Lucy. I better just keep quiet.*

Chapter 17

Uninvited Guests

Hugo and Amparo Medina threw a big party for the neighborhood on a Sunday afternoon in late August. Children of all ages swarmed around the yard, as the Medina house overflowed with neighbors. The oppressive tropical heat of late summer was in full force, and the neighborhood dressed in shorts and light cottons for the occasion. Lucy's grandmother wore a white dress with a big red hibiscus pinned to it and, as always, she had on her big, floppy straw hat.

Mike wandered around thinking about his other friends. *It would be great if they could be the special guests. I could stand at the edge of the water and they could jump and spin. Everyone would gather around, and the dolphins and I could put on a show.*

Ophelia, the woman who worked at Mrs. Medina's big house, placed platters of food on long tables lined up on the patio. Two large punch bowls, one of red sangria and the other of white sangria, sat on the kitchen counter. Lemons, limes, and oranges floated in Hugo's signature wine concoction. The kids helped themselves to glasses of lemonade and fruit punch.

"Hugo," a lady in a bright yellow dress grabbed his arm, "you must give me the recipe for this wonderful sangria."

"Ah, Linda, it is a family secret, and if I gave it to you, you might not come back to my home to enjoy it." The two neighbors smiled at each other.

The two-story pale pink house, with its red tile roof and white shutters, stood out against the light blue of the bay. The glass doors led out to the back patio where the land began to narrow. The Medina house stood on its own little island, connected to Key Biscayne by an arched bridge made of coral rock.

Hugo and Paul fried fish in the yard over by the dock. A large metal pot stood on top of a black metal stand. Blue flames leaped around the pot. A group of men stood around the fish fryer, scooping chunks of brown fried fish out of the pot and onto platters lined with paper towels. Rusty grabbed two of the hot cubes of fish and tossed one to Mike.

Jim spoke quietly. "We could've been lost. We made it back to Nassau just in time. The pumps couldn't keep up with the leaks and the water pouring in. And Mike's survival—well—a miracle."

Hugo nodded. The men sipped on their brown bottles of Pabst Blue Ribbon beer.

"You should see *Las Olas*. She's a mess, I had to have her towed back to Miami."

The delightful sounds of talking and laughing filled the air as the crowd ate, drank, and buzzed about. A few of the "almost eighth-grade" girls stood by the bay in animated conversation. Some others played badminton. The little red ball with its feathers floated over the net with agonizing slowness. Someone would swing their racket and miss. No one kept score. A few boys threw a football around.

Laughing hysterically, a woman dressed in pink pedal pushers twirled a red hula-hoop around her waist. She moved her hips and backside around in a circular motion, trying to keep the hoop spinning. It spun two or three times and clattered to the ground. Two young boys had the hula-hoops whizzing around them with ease.

Lucy's grandmother put her hand on Mike's shoulder.

It startled Mike as he watched a speed boat floating out in the bay.

"Hello, Miguel, are you going to have some of my coconut ice cream today?"

"Oh, yes, Ma'am. Lots of it."

"Good for you," she said with a gentle smile.

Over in the corner of the yard, Carmen's helper, Francisco, turned the crank on top of Mrs. Medina's famous ice cream maker.

Watching the party, two men with binoculars sat in a boat far out in the bay.

"What do you think?" The man put his glasses down. A deep scar ran across his right cheek from just under his eye to below his ear. The other man, Rico, continued to peer through his binoculars.

"I think it should be easy."

"If we go in there, we'll need to be very quiet with the boat." Eddie said. "If they hear us, we got a problem."

Rico put his binoculars down. "If they hear us, they got a problem." Both men laughed. Rico started the engine and piloted the boat back toward Miami. They headed north and west, into the mouth of the Miami River. Crowding both sides of the river, big fishing boats, old island tramp steamers, and shrimp boats floated in water the color of cloudy, dark tea. The smells of old fish, seaweed, and oil mixed together.

Eddie and Rico pulled between a wooden shrimp boat and the towering, black, rusty steel hull of an old freighter. Oil oozed out of its dilapidated hull and caused the surface of the water around the ship to glisten with an iridescent green and purple film.

Eddie and Rico's little boat fit under the dock. The two made sure to hide it from curious observers, both on the dock and out on the river. They tied up, climbed a metal ladder, and walked between two old wooden warehouses to the street. Across the street, Eddie opened the doors to a garage containing a big, black Buick. They paid an old man ten dollars a month for the garage and no questions asked.

Rico and Eddie rode to a little stucco building in a run-down neighborhood on Miami Beach. The boss lived there in an apartment furnished with a couch, two chairs, a TV, and a folding card table. The two thugs knew the boss worked for someone else. They didn't know who, and they didn't care. They liked the pay for not doing much—not much, so far.

After trudging up three flights of stairs, Rico knocked on the door. It opened just a little, with the chain stretched across the opening. The door closed, the chain came off, and the door opened. The boss sat down at the card table.

"How are you guys doing?"

"It's done. It's perfect," Rico said. "The rum runners who built that place back in the '20s knew what they were doing. We had to do a little repair work. You know the old guy who said he built it and used it as a hideout? He died in a car accident a couple of weeks ago. Now we think we're the only people who know about it."

Carlos nodded his approval. "Are you sure you can't see it?"

Eddie said, "We checked it out from every angle."

"Did you check it at night with some lights on?"

"Sure we did—no way to see anything. I had Rico flash some lights and lanterns while I rode around in the boat out in the bay. Nothing comes out of that swamp."

Rico opened the refrigerator and got out three beers. "We bought the lumber for cash from a guy in Fort Lauderdale and the hut has got tar paper covering almost every inch of it. It's almost invisible. We didn't touch a tree in that swamp."

"Can you see the channel from the bay?" Carlos asked.

"The channel is maybe eight to ten feet wide, and we got mangrove branches that slide across the opening," Eddie said. "There are seventy-five miles of mangrove swamp down there. No one will ever find that hut."

Behind the couch, Carlos picked up a black leather bag. He flopped it on the card table, reached in, and pulled out an automatic pistol. He tucked the gun into his belt as Eddie and Rico drank their beers. Carlos pulled out a wad of bills and counted out two piles. "Here you go, boys. This should keep you going."

The two thugs picked up the money and smiled. Carlos had been generous with them.

"Remember our deal. If we don't do anything, you each get five thousand. If we have to snatch her, you get twenty apiece when you do it and twenty each when it's over."

Rico and Eddie nodded.

Carlos handed them a piece of paper. "Call me at this number every night at nine. It's a pay phone, so let it ring. Just hang around Miami and don't get into any trouble."

"How long do you think we'll be waiting?" Eddie asked.

"We got at least a few months. And remember, I'll pay your expenses. I'm guessing nothing is going to happen, and you two will end up with the easiest five grand you ever made, and that'll be it."

The two men walked out. Once outside, Rico muttered, "You know, Eddie, I'd love to know who this guy is working for."

"Who cares? We're doing pretty good." Eddie slapped Rico on the back, and they got into the black Buick. "Let's go have some fun."

Chapter 18
Discovery

The three brothers rode together the first day of school. "Mike," warned Bob, "remember you've got Mrs. Aronsen this year. Watch out."

"She's nice, but she gets mean if you got ants in your pants or talk too much," Will added.

"I won't have to worry about that," Mike said.

"Yeah," Bob and Will both laughed. "Just remember," Bob said, "she always carries a yardstick around with her. She'll rap you with it from behind."

"She never raps the girls," Will said.

That first day of school, Mike did something he had never done before. Every morning, the children stood and recited The Pledge of Allegiance. Mike always moved his lips but never said the words out loud. Instead he would say the Pledge in his head. Today he put his hand over his heart and said aloud:

"I pledge allegiance to the flag of the United States of America, and to the Republic, for which it stands, one Nation, under God, indivisible, with liberty and justice for all."

He recited the words perfectly. No one in the room noticed what Mike had done.

I'll never forget this, the pledge, the first time, thought Mike.

After introducing herself and going over the sixth grade rules, Mrs. Aronsen began the day. "This morning, class, we're going to have a little fun. We're going to have a spelling bee using last year's vocabulary words. I'm sure you have remembered the words. Let me review the rules. We will pick two teams. I'll call out the words, alternating from one team to the other. If you miss a word, you must sit down. The team with the last person standing wins. The winning team gets a treat at lunch." Mrs. Aronsen pointed to a tray of chocolate cupcakes sitting on a table in the corner.

Mrs. Aronsen picked two captains. They took turns picking the teams and lined up on opposite sides of the room. The students whispered in the ears of the captains, helping them pick the best spellers for their team. Mike sat at his desk; he ended up as the last person chosen.

Mrs. Aronsen sat behind her desk and called out the words:

"Alternative."

"Efficiency."

"Inflammable."

"Language."

"Coronation."

"Procrastinate."

Children missed words and sat down. Each side lost a few students on the first round. Mike's turn came and Mrs. Aronsen gave him a word.

"Temporary," she said.

Mike answered, "T-e-m-p-o-r-a-r-y."

Almost no one noticed that Mike had not only spelled the word correctly, but also hadn't stuttered. Molly Davis, a classmate of Mike's since first grade, stood next to him. She gave Mike a huge grin. Mike smiled back.

The contest continued, and soon only two students stood facing each other: Mike and Norma Cahill. Mrs. Aronsen walked around to the front of her desk. She rapped her yardstick on the desk in front of her. "Children, I want complete silence. No one must say a word. I don't want anyone trying to help."

She turned to Norma. "Norma, the word is adjournment."

Norma blinked, "A–j–o–u–r–n–m–e–n–t."

"I'm sorry, Norma. That is incorrect."

The children on Mike's team cheered. "No, wait, children. Mike must now spell the word that Norma missed."

Mrs. Aronsen turned to Mike. "Mike, spell adjournment."

"A–d–j–o–u–r–n–m–e–n–t."

"Mike, that is correct."

The children cheered again.

"Quiet, class. Let me remind you that if Mike spells the next word correctly, his team wins. If not, then Norma gets another chance. Mike, your word is 'miscellaneous'."

The class mumbled—it was a tough word.

"Quiet please." Mrs. Aronsen rapped her yardstick on her desk.

Norma smiled.

"Miscellaneous." Mike paused. "M-i-s-c-e-l-l-a-n-e-o-u-s."

"That's right," Mrs. Aronsen said.

Mike's team jumped up and shouted. Patting and slapping Mike on the back, they crowded around him. Mrs. Aronsen tapped her yardstick lightly on the blackboard. "Okay, students. Settle down and take your seats." Mrs. Aronsen walked over to Mike. "Mike, congratulations on your performance." She spoke to the class, "I want all of you to remember that this morning the last person chosen ended up being the person who won the spelling bee. I hope this makes you stop and think about how we judge or misjudge people."

Not moving, Mike sat at his desk. He could feel the eyes of the whole class on him. He knew the right answers to the questions most of the time, but in the past, he had never raised his hand. He never wanted to stutter through the answers. Now he knew he could raise his hand like everybody else.

Mike sped home after school, beating Bob, Will, and the others.

"Mom, Mom!"

Mike burst through the front door.

"What is it, Mike?" Alice walked in from the kitchen.

"Mom, I won the spelling bee. My team won and I spelled the last word!"

"That's fantastic, Mike!" She gave her son a big hug.

"Can I have some chocolate milk?"

"Sure." Alice stirred the milk, and Mike chugged it down. Bob and Will walked in the front door.

"Did you hear about your brother?"

"Yeah," Bob said, "last one picked and the last one standing. Way to go, Mike."

"You got picked last, Mike?"

"It's no big deal, Mom."

Will and Bob leaned in the kitchen doorway. "Well, no one will pick you last again."

"I want you boys to start your homework now, or no TV tonight."

Mike took his books and walked out to the table on the dock. He scribbled in his math notebook a little, but his mind wandered to that faraway place under the ocean floor. Then he felt a slight mental prod. Down the inlet dorsal fins moved toward him.

Hi, Mike, Naarin said.

How was school today? Shanti greeted him.

Great. I won the spelling bee.

What's a spelling bee? Shanti asked.

Hey, Uncle Malak, Risa, do you know what a spelling bee is?

No, Naarin, I don't.

Nope, said Risa.

It's a contest where the teacher calls out a word and you have to spell it, Mike explained.

Nyla, Naar, Corran, Loa, and a few others joined them. Nyla didn't think much of the spelling bee. *Since we can't read or write, spelling is something we would never be interested in.*

We would *be interested in listening to another book, when you're ready, Mike,* Corran said.

I don't have one with me now, but I'll...

"Hey, Mike, what are you doing?"

Will had slipped around the house and walked over behind the old silver boat on the ramp. Eshu, Risa, Shanti and big Malak swam next to the ramp near the dock. Will walked toward the dock as the dolphins slipped below the surface.

Mike jumped a little but made an effort to turn around.

It's your brother, Nyla said.

Please don't go.

We must go. It's not wise for us to stay here.

As she slipped away, Loa said, *Remember, Mike, we don't want to make it more difficult for you to keep the secret.*

"The dolphins are cool. I wish they wouldn't go away."

Mike stood still and peered into the water. "Yeah, they're great. I like them."

"Well, the neat thing is that they seem to like you. Have you figured out what they're saying?"

Mike jerked his head around toward Will. A shock ran through his body.

"Huh?"

"You know—when they screech and squeak. You got any idea what they're trying to say?"

"Uh—uh—no. I guess they're just calling out to each other."

"Yeah, Bob and I think they're coming up here to be near you."

"Nah. They're just swimming around. Maybe they just feel safe up here."

"Yeah, well Mr. Higgins says they never stop down at his dock. He says the dolphins swim past his dock and swim up here to our dock all the time."

Mike just shrugged his shoulders and tried to control his emotions.

"You know, Mr. Higgins has re-named the inlet 'Dolphin Cut'. He says the dolphins never came up here when he first moved in. Now they're up here almost every day. Mom noticed it too. You should go get some bait fish and try feeding them. They might come around even more. Like I said, Bob and I think they're coming to see you, like that time at the Beach Club." Will turned toward the house. "I'm going inside to do my homework."

Mike sat down. His stomach churned.

The next day, Mrs. Aronsen assigned the usual essay that required each child to describe his or her summer. Mike got an A on his. Mrs. Aronsen had Mike read his essay in front of the class. Without stumbling over a single word, Mike read about catching the great sailfish, being given the painting, and his brother's encounter with the barracuda. The children were mesmerized by Mike's tale of the storm at sea, and being rescued by Darius. His classmates cheered and clapped as Mike described his return to Nassau and his reunion with his dad. He ended by holding up his painting and explaining that it now hung in his room as his most prized possession. Standing in the back of the classroom, Mrs. Pomerance and Miss Woodward listened to Mike and smiled through the entire reading. As he finished, Mike acknowledged the two ladies with a slight nod and a wave. He sat down grinning from ear to ear. He wondered what would have happened if he had told the real story.

As the weeks went by, Mike raised his hand constantly. Sometimes he just yelled out answers. At first he reveled in this, but he soon realized that blurting out the answers wasn't such a good idea. Others needed a chance to answer. Mike knew the importance of being smart and doing his best. In the time that he had stuttered, he kept quiet because of the embarrassment. Now he chose to think and listen. He had never made that choice before.

In early January, the warm sun attracted many folks from up north, and visitors crowded the Key.

Bob, Will, Mike, Rusty, Diane, and Lucy walked their bikes out of the back gate at school. Rusty asked, "Hey, Lucy, can we fish off your bridge?"

"You can if you want. I've got to go to a piano lesson."

"We'll get the rods from our garage," Bob announced.

"Rusty, you got any bait?" Will asked.

"Yeah, my dad's got some shrimp in the freezer."

"Great. We'll meet you on the bridge." Will jumped on his bike.

A black Buick slowed almost to a stop on the street. The kids had to push their bikes around the car as it paused in the crosswalk. No one paid much attention except Mike.

Mike glanced at the two men in the front seat. They pretended not to watch, but Mike knew they were watching. *I think I've seen this car around the Key, but I'm not sure. These men are watching me. Maybe they know something about the dolphins. Maybe they are skwill from the under Seegans. I better ask the dolphins.*

As the car drove away Mike saw one of the men looking back at them.

Most afternoons, Mike went out on the dock to sit at the table and do his homework. Some days, the dolphins came. Now they seemed to be swimming around the inlet more and more. Different groups floated in on different days. Mike came to the realization that if the dolphins thought that they would be seen by people along the inlet, they would not swim up to visit him. Mike had asked about skwill being on the Key and the dolphins had reported that there were none from Krondal's ship stationed anywhere near the Key. Mike worried about skwill from the under Seegans, but he hadn't seen the black Buick again since that day near school.

As they did on many days, several dolphins floated near his dock waiting for Mike to come home after school.

Hi, Mike, Eshu said first.

Hi, who's out there?

Oh, it's me, Corran, along with Loa, Eshu, Malak, and two of our friends from down south.

Eshu said, *Mike, how about reading to us?*

Yeah, read something.

Yeah, Mike.

Okay, I'll be right back. I have a great book about a boy named Tom Sawyer. Mike ran to the house, came back with the book, and began to read.

Corran rolled over in the water. *That is wonderful, Mike. You know, we have many stories that we can tell you. Our ancestors have passed them down to us.*

Yes, our Teachers have given us the power to remember them word for word.

Just like the way you remember the books? Mike asked.

Yes, for hundreds of years these stories have been passed down from generation to generation. We carry the legends of ancient Indians, pirates, hidden treasure, and great sea battles, Corran said.

Mike latched on to an idea. *Do you know where there's buried treasure?*

Once, an ancestor of ours showed the first person who could ever talk to us where a treasure lay hidden in an underwater cave.

Some of our friends helped Archie find an old sailing ship not too long ago, Malak said.

Could you show me *where there is buried treasure?*

Well, Malak said, *we can't tell you what happens on land when we lose sight of the people. But we know the location of most of the sunken ships and gold coins in the sea.*

We can see the ships that sunk hundreds of years ago and are now covered with sand and coral, said Loa.

How can you do that?

We send out sound waves. The sound bounces off an object and comes back to us and then we can visualize the object. It is a great talent, Loa said.

It comes in very handy at night, Malak said.

Is it the squeaking sounds you make?

No, it's a clicking sound you would hear if you put your head in the water. And, you would also feel it. The next time you're in the water at the cove, we'll show you.

Corran slapped his tail fluke on the water. *Mike, find something—something small to throw in the water.*

Mike stood up and reached in his pocket. He held up a nickel. *How about this?*

Sure. Now, throw it as far as you can down the inlet.

Turning, Mike threw the coin as far as he could. He barely saw it hit the water.

Go get it, Eshu, Corran said.

Ha, no problem, Eshu said, as he rose out of the water, spun, and blasted down the inlet. In less than a minute he swam past the dock, pulled up at the boat ramp, and rested his head on the concrete ramp. The coin fell from his mouth. Mike stared at the coin, dumbfounded.

"Wow," he said quietly, but out loud, "Wow."

And remember, Mike, we can find that coin anytime, anywhere. Corran said.

Even at night?

Oh yes. Even at night.

Seeing with sound, Malak said, *gives us a great advantage over other creatures, especially when seeing with your eyes is impossible. It's how some of us helped Archie find the German submarines.*

Archie? Submarines? Tell me. Please, tell me that story.

Come on, Malak. Not now. We have to go. You shouldn't do this, Loa said.

No, wait. Tell me about the Indians, the pirates, the treasure, the submarines.

Almost crazy with excitement, Mike walked back and forth on the dock.

The stories are so long, Corran said. *When we are at the cove, we will tell you. There is plenty of time.*

Loa turned to leave. *Come on, we should go.*

Good-bye, Mike.

See you soon, Mike.

Good-bye, everyone.

As the dolphins swam out toward the bay, Mike stood on his dock until they disappeared. He started toward his house and just then he saw it—the big floppy straw hat behind a tree. Mike turned back but he didn't see anything—or did he?

Chapter 19
Special Cargo

Hugo Medina's father had moved to Miami from Colombia twenty-five years earlier and bought most of the island of Key Biscayne, where he planted hundreds of coconut palms. The family's wealth, however, derived from their successful and profitable shipping business, and not their hobby of growing coconuts.

After his father died, Hugo expanded the company. Big blue ships with MEDINA emblazoned in white letters on their sides sailed throughout the Caribbean carrying vehicles, machinery, and industrial equipment to various countries in South America, and bringing back lumber, fruit, and cloth.

With the excitement of the storm, Mike's near-fatal adventure behind him, and *Las Olas* repaired, Hugo relaxed on this voyage down to Colombia. He liked to sail on his cargo ships, because the trips always gave him time to think.

Standing on the bridge of the big freighter, Hugo chatted with the ship's captain, Rich Turner. Rich hailed from Port Arthur, Texas, and had been on convoy duty during the war. Around the ports of South America, Rich knew how to handle himself, his ship, and the people on the docks.

Hugo sipped on a cup of strong coffee and surveyed the deck of the ship. Industrial machinery, two bulldozers, and a dozen school buses filled the deck in orderly, closely-packed rows.

"How does she handle with this heavy equipment on board, Rich?"

"Not bad, this ship is steady. Next trip, I hear we're bringing down some military equipment, tanks, and heavy guns."

"Yeah, for the Peruvian government, compliments of Uncle Sam. Uncle Sam is even paying for the shipping."

"When we load that stuff, we'll have to pack it much deeper in the ship."

Hugo nodded, "Where are the gifts?"

Rich motioned over his shoulder. "In my cabin. I got a case of scotch for the harbor pilot. I want to get us into one of the best slips closest to the exit gates. We need to move these buses off the waterfront and into secure parking as fast as we can. We also have a couple of high-priced cars below. They can't sit around for even ten minutes."

Hugo nodded in agreement. "Get the boys to move those gifts down to the gangway as soon as we dock."

"Sure, boss. What are we bringing back this time?"

"A load of mahogany and teak; it should fill the ship."

"That exotic wood is selling pretty well, huh?"

"Yeah. I hope they never run out of it down here," Hugo said, as he began walking back to his cabin.

For Hugo, an ominous cloud hung over this trip. Bernardo Gonzalez, the Colombian secretary of the interior, had requested a meeting. Gonzalez had been in the government for many years, and most insiders considered him to be as powerful as the president of Colombia. Hugo had met Gonzalez once before, at the government offices in Bogotá, when his father had introduced them. After that meeting, Hugo's father told him to be wary of Gonzalez, and never trust him.

In the dawn, the huge ship inched closer to the dock, now a few feet away. Hugo walked onto the bridge holding a mug of coffee as Rich leaned over a railing on the bridge.

"Good morning, Rich."

"Good morning, Hugo, how did you sleep?"

"Just fine."

Rich pointed, "What's that about?" Wearing olive drab military fatigues, two men leaned against a black limousine parked at the edge of the dock.

"I guess that's my ride."

"What do you mean?"

"I've got a meeting with a government big shot. He said he'd send somebody to pick me up."

"When will you be back?"

"Probably late this afternoon; I've got to go to this guy's house out in the country."

"That's a little strange. You want somebody to go with you?"

"No, Rich, it's okay, but let's be ready to head back as soon as we can."

"We'll, be ready to go in the morning."

"That's fine Rich." Hugo forced a smile.

The thick green vegetation grew up to the edge of the road, and the big black limousine swerved to miss pot holes in the road as it climbed the mountain trail. Now and then the green wall broke open, and Hugo could see down onto a tree-covered valley below. Not a building or road could be seen in any direction. Countless birds, with their vibrant colors of red, blue, yellow, and white outlined against the dark green, perched and flew among the tree tops.

Turning off the pavement and onto a gravel road, the car pulled up to a stone archway and a closed iron gate. Ceramic tile letters across the top of the entrance spelled out CASA ESCONDIDA.

The limo rolled slowly through the gates and up the narrow path. They then pulled onto a taupe stone courtyard that spread out, flat, and slick with dampness. The house, made of the same slate stone, sprawled up at the end of the courtyard. Lacquered mahogany shutters and window frames added richness to the building. Green algae stained the red, brown, and maroon barrel tiles of the roof, and a foggy mist hung in the air.

When the limo stopped in front of the house, Hugo stepped out. A few strides brought him to heavy wooden doors with rings of brass hanging in the middle. One of the doors opened and a large man in a military uniform stepped back to let him pass.

"Hugo," A voice boomed from inside the house. A heavyset man with his black hair slicked back and a short trimmed black mustache walked toward him. "I hope your drive was comfortable."

"Yes, Señor Gonzalez, it was pleasant."

"Please, Hugo—Bernardo, just Bernardo." The two men shook hands. "Welcome to Casa Escondida."

They walked toward the back of the house, through an entrance area paneled in rich woods. A stairway curved up on the left to the second floor, and polished terracotta tile stretched throughout the house.

"Your home is beautiful," Hugo said.

"Thank you. I had it built about ten years ago. Even though this house is out in the country, I have every modern convenience. Your father visited here just after I finished it."

"Yes, I remember him speaking of it."

The two men stepped down into a large living room. Ceiling to floor glass panels curved outward showcasing a patio and swimming pool made of the same stone as the courtyard. The dark stone in the pool gave the water a deep blue color. Beyond the pool, the jungle had been cut away to reveal another mountain rising across a valley of lush rainforest.

Walking out around the pool to the far side of the patio, the two men came to a table covered with a white cloth and perched precariously close to the edge of the patio. A silver coffeepot and two white cups sat on the table.

Hugo saw that the jungle floor dropped away and fell almost straight down. He could hear the sound of falling water nearby, and mist and fog veiled the green expanse that stretched off to the horizon. "Please, Hugo," Bernardo motioned for Hugo to sit down. "Coffee?"

"Yes, thank you."

As Bernardo served the coffee, Hugo listened to the sounds of the jungle, and could only identify a few of the cries, squawks, and chirps. A long, gangly monkey hung on a branch where the jungle grew up to the patio.

"So, Hugo, how is your business doing?"

"Very well. Our shipping company has contracts with many governments to ship military equipment to South America. We are buying and selling a lot of products and equipment here in Colombia and in Venezuela," Hugo smiled. "Thanks to your department, we will be shipping you a lot of road-building equipment this year. We greatly appreciate the business."

Bernardo nodded. "It's no problem. Medina Shipping has always done more than expected. What did you bring down this time?"

"Oh, some industrial machinery, a few bulldozers, some cars, and a dozen school buses."

"Yes, yes, the school buses. I heard some people in the Education Ministry talking about them. What will you be taking back?"

"A load of mahogany and teak. I have it sold to some furniture manufacturers and yacht builders in the states."

"Well, we have plenty of trees here." He waved toward the valley and mountains around them. "You had a crazy experience with that hurricane this summer, eh, Hugo?"

"It was pretty scary. The young son of one of my neighbors was washed overboard, but, thanks to God, he survived without a scratch."

"Yes, I heard. Truly a miracle."

Bernardo leaned over the table. "Hugo, I asked you to come to here because I need to continue to do some special business with you. I'm sure you know that your father and I had an arrangement for many years."

"Bernardo, I know our company has shipped and handled hundreds of items for the government, but I'm not sure—"

Bernardo stopped him. "The special crates your father shipped for me contained items of a personal and confidential nature. No other company can do this but yours. It is also very profitable." Bernardo smiled at Hugo and got up from the table. He motioned to Hugo. "Come. I want to show you something."

The two men walked toward the house.

Bernardo came to a door in the kitchen. He opened it and started down a spiral stairway to the basement. A few tools hung on a peg board. Wooden shelving stood against another wall and on the far side of the room stood a lone cabinet. Walking up to this cabinet, Bernardo tugged on one side. The cabinet scraped on the floor as it swung open to reveal a dark tunnel entrance.

Hugo kept his calm façade as his eyes darted back and forth, his stomach fluttered, and his palms moistened. Bernardo flipped a switch. When the light came on, Hugo squinted into the narrow tunnel. Curving out of sight, the tunnel bent down at a steep angle. A damp, musty, mildew smell hung in the air. With his shoulders rubbing against the rough hewn stone, the big man walked down in front of Hugo, and as Bernardo came to a wooden door, he opened it.

Hugo followed Bernardo onto a tiny outdoor landing; he looked up through the dense foliage and saw the edge of the patio. Hugo realized that the tunnel had been dug below the pool and patio, and led to a narrow foot path, cut into the sheer cliff, below the house. *But why?*

On the path, the men pushed branches and vines aside, as they inched toward another wooden door secured by a steel grate and built flush into the stone face of the cliff.

Bernardo opened the creaking grate and unlocked the door. He pulled on a cord; a string of light bulbs came on, and they stepped inside. The natural cave widened as it went into the mountain. Hugo hesitated behind Bernardo, as his eyes darted in every direction. Roots from the jungle trees had burrowed into the cave and had been cut away. The sound of dripping water splashed on the stone floor.

"Bernardo, I don't understand. Where are we?" Hugo said, "and what—"

"Just a minute, my friend," Bernardo cut him off. "You'll see." The word "friend" rang in Hugo's ear. He would never consider Bernardo Gonzalez a friend.

Bernardo flipped another switch. Lights illuminated the cavern. In front of Hugo sat a thick stone table, upon which a foot high gold statue of a man stood, shining so brightly that it glowed. Next to it, a two-foot-long gold panther with black onyx eyes crouched, seemingly ready to strike. Hugo gasped and turned to his right. A gold platter, the size of a car tire, propped up on another stone table, glistened. Many of the artifacts mimicked actors on a stage, as directed white beams from spot lights located high up in the cave shone down on the ancient figurines.

"What do you think of my collection?" Bernardo said, his voice echoing in the cavern. Speechless, Hugo walked further into the cave and saw an unimaginable collection of ancient stone carvings, pottery, painted bowls, and jewelry. In a corner stood a square stone carving of a woman, twice Hugo's size, with her arms reaching out toward him.

"Amazing. I can't believe it, there is so much."

"I knew you would be impressed."

Tunnels led away from the main room. Many more carved pieces peered out of the darkness at Hugo. He knew these ancient artifacts were invaluable and must have been looted from archeological sites in the jungles of South America. He returned to the table in the center of the cavern. The gold figure stared at him with dark green sparkling eyes—eyes fashioned from penny-sized emeralds.

Gonzalez walked up to Hugo. "For years your father helped me ship many of these artifacts out of the country. I haven't shipped anything since his death, and now I need you to take all of this to the States, as soon as possible."

"Bernardo," Hugo gestured around the room, "these are some of the national treasures of Colombia, and I'm sure, some of these artifacts have come from other countries in the region. This is highly illegal and could be dangerous."

Bernardo smiled. "Nonsense, the peasants don't care, and remember that I am the Minister of the Interior. I control what happens here. No one will inspect the crates. No one will question you."

Hugo forced a smile and nodded his head in agreement. He knew continuing this conversation would be foolish.

As the two men walked back to the house, Hugo remained quiet and uncomfortable, and the conversation became decidedly one way. "You know, Hugo, there is an incredible demand for this type of ancient art, and pieces like those are laying all over the jungles down here. I have men searching constantly." The men stood in the foyer and Bernardo put his hand on Hugo's shoulder. "When your next ship arrives, we will be ready. I expect you to personally supervise the loading and unloading of the boxes. Remember, you will be handsomely rewarded."

Hugo sat on the bridge, as the coast of Colombia disappeared behind him.

"You're quiet this morning," Rich said.

"Just thinking. Say, Rich, when my dad came down here, did he ever ship back some crates that never got on the ship's manifest?"

"Yep. Once or twice a year when he rode down. He said he needed to do a few favors for some friends. I figured they just wanted to slip around some of those stupid taxes they have down here. Why are you asking? Do we have a problem?"

"No—no problem."

Hugo spent a lot of time thinking as he sailed back to Miami. He could not imagine why his father had made the illegal shipments. Hugo knew his father did not like Gonzalez. His father had told him that Gonzalez possessed much power and authority and must be tolerated, but he should never be trusted. Hugo knew that if he refused to ship the artifacts, Medina Shipping would have a hard time doing business in Colombia in the future.

By the time they had sailed back to Miami, Hugo had made up his mind. He would refuse to ship the ancient treasures.

The day after he returned, he went to his office and telephoned Colombia. Bernardo Gonzalez sounded cheerful. "Hello, Hugo, how was your trip back?"

"Just fine, Bernardo."

"When will you be back?"

"Oh, in about two weeks."

"Good, good. We'll have dinner together when you're here."

"Señor Gonzalez," Hugo paused and took a breath. "I must tell you that I cannot ship the special goods you have requested."

The silence on the other end of the line made Hugo even more nervous; then Gonzalez spoke in a quiet, firm voice. "Hugo, I do not have time to hire another shipper, and Medina Shipping is never inspected. You must do this."

"I'm sorry, Señor. The times have changed. Your government and the governments of many of your neighboring countries have become serious about losing their antiquities. This would be a serious International crime."

Bernardo Gonzalez started to raise his voice. "Hugo, remember, I am the government and the rest of the peasants down here do not care about these things. Your family made a lot of money doing this, and I assure you, it will be no problem."

"Bernardo, my answer is still no."

"Hugo, I suggest you take a little more time to think about it."

Hugo spoke in a firm and quiet tone. "Señor Gonzalez, I know my family was involved in this in the past. I will not tell anyone what I saw."

"I know you won't." The line went dead.

Chapter 20

Mangroves

Every day at noon, Carlos waited by the pay phone. If the phone failed to ring in fifteen minutes, he walked away. Most days, it didn't ring. Today the phone rang. "Yes, Señor, yes. We have been ready for weeks. It will be no problem. They have their instructions. It may take a few days until we get an opportunity."

Friday after school, Mike walked across the coconut grove to the cove. He decided not to bring a book with him. He just hoped some of his friends would be lounging around in the secluded water. Mike saw two spotted dolphins speeding into the cove. They skimmed inches above the water and then slid back. The two zoomed up to the beach, and then turned away, splashing water up toward Mike.

Hi, Mike.

Hey, Mike.

Hello. Mike said, happy to see any of them.

My name's Pike and he's Finn. We swam into the bay a while ago and decided to come over and see if you were here and what you were doing.

Pike, didn't you help me catch a sailfish over toward Nassau a while back?

Yep, and the two of us helped Salvador and Riley pull you to Darius's island during the hurricane. We were worried that you might drown.

Gee, I guess I didn't know that you two had helped. Thanks… thanks a lot.

Not a problem, said Pike.

Have you seen Nyla and Naar lately?

Yeah, we saw them around the Bahamas a few days ago. We run into Nyla and Naar all the time, Finn said.

Salvador and Riley are our cousins, Pike added.

I hope I see them again, Mike said.

They'll be over here one day soon. We fish off the coast and come over to the bay to catch lobster. It's easy to get them near the lobster traps, said Finn.

Mike laughed out loud. *Better not let the lobstermen catch you robbing their traps.*

Oh, we don't actually go into the traps, Pike said. Anyway, you don't think they could catch us, do you?

Nope, not a chance.

We only eat the little ones, about the size of a big shrimp, Finn said. *The big ones are too hard to swallow.*

Mike and the two dolphins chatted about their friends and the sea for a while.

Mike stood at the waters edge. *I've got to get going guys. It's about time for dinner.*

Yeah, you're right Mike. I can hear those lobsters calling now, Finn said with a bit of a laugh. The dolphins swam out into the bay. *Good bye, Mike, see you around.*

Come back soon, Mike said, as he turned away from the cove.

Friday night dinner at the Connelly house usually consisted of some kind of fish with macaroni and cheese. Rusty joined them this evening and he sat at the table, spoon in hand, wolfing down huge mounds of the gooey yellow noodles. His sister, Diane, and a bunch of other girls had been invited to a slumber party at Lucy's house. The Medinas joined the Butlers for dinner at the Beachside Hotel while Carmen's housekeeper, Ophelia, stayed at Lucy's house to keep an eye on the girls. Lucy's parents never referred to Ophelia as a babysitter; Lucy would have disowned them.

After eating a few pounds of mac and cheese and a school of snapper, the four boys aimlessly hung around the garage at the Connelly's until Will disappeared and returned with two squirt guns firing away.

"Hey, cut it out, Will!" Rusty put up his hand in front of his face, but he still got wet. Mike threw a basketball at Will.

Bob's eyes twinkled. "We've got more squirt guns. Let's get them and sneak down to Lucy's."

"If we're real quiet, we can scare them," said Rusty.

Mike had already begun digging the plastic water pistols out of a box in the garage. "Hey guys, we have a bunch of them."

The boys filled the water guns and walked down the street. Mike squirted Rusty right in the ear as they walked over the bridge to the Medina house.

"Come on, Mike." Rusty rubbed his ear.

"Shhhhh," Bob whispered.

The boys slipped around to the back of the house. They tugged on the sliding glass door that led into the kitchen. Silently, the door opened, and the boys crept into the darkened house. At the end of a short hallway off the kitchen, Ophelia sat listening to a radio and reading by a little lamp next to her. The boys tiptoed through the kitchen.

Bob turned back to the others and whispered, "Okay, let's sneak around the stairs. I'll make some noise, and when they come downstairs, we'll get them." The boys grinned and nodded.

Upstairs, the girls played records while they talked. "Rock Around The Clock" blared out of the upstairs bedroom. Bob and the other boys made noises like dogs howling.

The girls came rushing out of the bedroom and down the stairs. Jumping out from behind the couches and around the corner, the boys sprang the trap. They fired their squirt guns, and sprayed their eager victims. The girls screamed and ran up the stairs back into Lucy's room. The door slammed shut and shrieks and laughter filled the house.

Ophelia came out of her room and playfully scolded the boys in Spanish. They understood little of Ophelia's tirade but knew they had better retreat.

Laughing, the boys ran out the back door.

As they ran over the bridge, Rusty said, "Did you see me get my sister?"

Alice stood on the front porch as the boys ran into the yard. "What have you boys been up to?" she said with mock sternness.

"We went down to Lucy's and scared the girls," Will said.

Alice smiled. "Well, it's getting late. Come on in, and leave those girls alone."

The boys walked inside and flopped on the floor in front of the television to catch the end of *Our Miss Brooks*.

Watching the house through binoculars, Eddie and Rico sat in their power boat on the bay. "If those kids keep wandering around, we'll never get in there," Eddie said in a low voice.

"Don't worry. It'll quiet down soon."

And, in a few minutes, the house did quiet down.

"Let's go, Rico," Eddie said, "just like we planned." The boat slipped under the stone bridge leading from the island to the Medina property and reached the dock. Eddie and Rico jumped out of the boat and ran to the back of the house. Dressed in black, they pulled their knit masks over their heads and entered the house through the open glass door in the kitchen.

The light from Ophelia's room barely illuminated the hallway and kitchen. Eddie and Rico walked down the hallway. Ophelia never had a chance to get out of her chair. Her eyes bulged in terror, as Rico slapped a piece of silver tape across her mouth. They pulled her up; Eddie cuffed her hands behind her, pushed her into a closet, wedged a chair under the doorknob, and turned off the light.

Upstairs, Lucy, Diane, Clara, and Jeannie, sprawled on Lucy's bed. As "Maybellene" blared from the record player, they heard another noise.

"The boys are back," Clara said.

Lucy jumped up. "I've got an idea." She dug around the bottom of her closet and pulled out a pink water pistol.

"Great," Diane said, "you got any more of those?"

"I think so. Try in the bottom of the closet."

The girls ran for the closet. Lucy snuck down the hallway to the bathroom, filled the squirt gun and tiptoed down the stairs. Darkness filled the quiet house as Lucy crept around the corner into the kitchen.

Lucy didn't see the man. He stepped out of the dark behind her. A canvas bag came down hard over her head. Continuing the motion, he swept her up in a powerful bear hug. Lucy screamed, but the bag muffled her cry. Rico held her tight. "Shut up or I'll hurt you." The two men muscled the squirming bag to the dock.

Outside, Eddie jumped into the boat, Rico handed Lucy down, and Eddie laid her on the floor of the boat. "Come on, let's get outa here," Eddie whispered. He wrapped a rope around the bag and Lucy's arms and then tied another rope around her ankles. By then, Rico had the boat untied and the engines rumbling. The grab had taken less than five minutes, and Rico and Eddie smiled at each other as Rico pushed the throttle forward. The boat roared out into the darkness of the bay.

Inside the house the girls moved down the stairs with their water pistols in hand. They skulked around the living room—nothing.

"I thought I heard Lucy a minute ago," Diane said. "Was that a boat starting up out back?"

"Whose boat would that be?" Jeannie asked.

"I don't know," Clara said. "How about in the den."

"They can't be over there, Lucy must have chased them outside." Diane motioned to the back door, and the girls moved into the kitchen. The only illumination came from the lights of downtown Miami reflecting off the bay.

The girls huddled close to each other in the almost darkness. Puzzled by the thumping sound they heard coming from the room off the kitchen, they walked toward the noise.

Clara turned on the light, and saw the chair wedged against the door.

She pulled away the chair and opened the door to find Ophelia standing there, with tape across her mouth and her hands behind her back.

The girls screamed.

They pulled Ophelia out of the closet. Diane tugged at the corner of the tape, and then she took a deep breath and tore it away. Ophelia burst out in a barrage of nearly incoherent Spanish. None of the girls understood her except Clara. Clara blurted out, "Oh my God! She said that two men came in the house and grabbed her. Where's Lucy?"

In an instant, the girls realized what had happened. Diane cried, "We've got to get help."

Scrambling out the front door, they ran over the bridge and down the street to the Connelly's house. The girls ran up to the house, stumbling over one another as they pushed through the door. Diane got through first and blurted out, sobbing, "Mr. Connelly, help! Somebody's taken Lucy!"

"Lucy's gone!" Jeannie screamed.

Clara burst out over Jeannie, "Some men came into the house and pushed Ophelia into a closet! She had tape on her mouth!"

Jim stood up. "What? Calm down. Stop crying."

Diane tried to catch her breath; she could barely speak. "What do we do?"

Jim turned to Alice. "Call the police and then the hotel." Jim ran out the front door, the children following him.

"Kids, stay here!" Alice shouted. They stopped in their tracks. "Get in this house." She dialed the phone.

"This is Alice Connelly on Harbor Drive.

"There has been some trouble over at the Medina house. We think someone kidnapped Lucy Medina.

"I don't know. My husband is going over there now. Please Hurry.

"He's already gone.

"Yes, please hurry." Alice hung up the phone.

"Kids, don't any of you leave this house." Alice found the number for the hotel and dialed.

"Hello. This is Alice Connelly.

"Mr. and Mrs. Hugo Medina are having dinner at the hotel with some friends. They are probably in the dining room or the bar. I need someone to find them and tell them there is an emergency and to come home immediately. Please hurry."

Alice hung up and started down the street. The children watched Alice hurry as they followed along toward the little bridge. Lights now shone from the windows of the Medina house.

Alice poked her head in the open front door. "Jim?"

Bob, now standing on the steps behind his mother caught her glare. "I told you to stay…"

"I'm back here, Alice." Jim's voice came from the back of the house.

Alice walked into the kitchen. Ophelia sobbed, as Jim stood behind her trying to spring the lock on the cuffs with a paring knife. "I can't get them off." He turned to Alice. "Did you get the police?"

"They're on the way."

"Ophelia, don't worry," Jim said, "the police will get these off."

"What happened?"

"As best I can figure, two men came in here and pushed Ophelia in a closet, and Lucy's missing."

Diane pointed down at the pink plastic water pistol laying on the kitchen floor. "I think that's the one Lucy had."

Three police cars from the village pulled up with their lights flashing, but without the sirens turned on. Two of the cars pulled around the drive; the other car stopped on the bridge and blocked it. Two policemen hurried into the house. The other officers walked around the house.

"What happened?" The policeman asked the group now standing in the front yard.

Diane spoke up. "We heard something. We figured the boys came back—Lucy went downstairs, and we heard her sorta scream."

"We heard a boat leave," Clara said. "Then we found Ophelia in the closet."

The policeman held up his hand. "Okay, stay here, please." He went to one of the cars and got on the radio. One of the Spanish-speaking policemen removed the handcuffs and knelt in front of Ophelia speaking to her quietly as she continued to sob.

The third policeman gathered the group together. "Folks, we'll need all of you to stay here until the detectives arrive. They're on the way."

Jim stood at the front door as Hugo's car pulled up on the bridge and his four neighbors hurried toward the house. Jim's eyes met Hugo's.

"Lucy's gone."

"What do you mean, gone?" Amparo said.

"Two men came into the house and pushed Ophelia in a closet and now Lucy is missing."

Amparo buried her head in her husband's chest and began crying. The color drained from Hugo's face.

Three police cars from Miami pulled up, followed by a dark blue sedan. Two detectives got out of the car and walked over the bridge, stopping to give some instructions to the uniformed policemen. They walked over to the crowd of kids and parents now gathered in the front yard. Both men wore dark blue suits, white shirts, and dark ties. One had a short stocky body and was almost bald. The other stood a little taller and had a thick head of black hair peppered with a bit of silver. "I'm Tony Galdo and this is Lou Verdona, we're detectives with the Miami Police Department. Where are the Medinas?" said the shorter detective. His accent gave away his New York City origin and Italian heritage.

"Right here," Hugo said, as the couple stepped over to the detectives.

"Folks, we have police boats and the Coast Guard in the bay now," Lou said, "We'll find Lucy. Mr. Medina, Can you think of anyone who would want to harm you or your family?"

"No, I don't know of anybody."

"How about you Mrs. Medina?" Lou asked.

Amparo shook her head as she sobbed in her husband's arms.

"I'd like the kids and parents to stay out front until we search the house, and then we'll go into the living room," announced Galdo. He turned to a uniformed policeman, "Ortega, go in and question the housekeeper. She doesn't speak English and she might be our only witness."

"Will Lucy be okay?" asked Mike.

"Sure," Tony Galdo said. "These people don't want to harm her, they just want money." He patted Mike on the shoulder.

Mike's mind raced. *She's my best friend. I know she's older than me but she's still my best friend. She's got to be okay.*

The two detectives questioned the boys. They hadn't heard or seen anything. The girls didn't give the detectives any useful information either, except the part about the boat roaring away from the dock.

"There will be a policeman here tonight." Lou said. "If anyone thinks of anything, or if anyone is contacted, tell the officer on duty. We'll be back in the morning. Mr. and Mrs. Medina, we will do everything possible to get your daughter back safe and sound."

Mike walked behind the others as they went home. He stopped on the bridge and looked back into the black bay. *Where is she? She's got to be okay. I wish I could talk to her. I wish she could hear my mind. She's just got to be okay.*

Far to the south, Eddie and Rico crept up to the edge of the mangrove swamp in their boat. Lucy lay on the floor in the canvas bag.

On this cloudy moonless night, the darkness concealed them, and as they floated into the mangroves, it became even darker. Branches hung over the men and scraped the sides of the boat as it squeezed into the narrow inlet. With the craft now enveloped by the mangroves, Eddie walked to the stern and pulled a branch across the narrow channel, hiding the opening. The boat crept thirty feet into the swamp before the channel grew a little wider and turned sharply to the left. They moved slowly, taking another sharp turn back to the right, before Rico turned on a flashlight and pointed it toward the shack.

Mosquitoes, sand fleas, gnats, and flies swarmed around the boat. The low, gurgling rumble of the boat's engine and the buzzing of insects broke the silence of the black swamp.

Four wood pilings held the rickety hut out of the water, and the roof slanted to one side. The builders of the hut had constructed the hideout around the mangrove trees, and branches grew through the floor and roof. The windows, covered with tattered screens, had no glass. The narrow dock ran along the side of the inlet up to the hut, and sat just above the black water. A ladder with four steps led from the dock up to a porch that surrounded the entire hut. Long pieces of wood nailed to the pilings in each corner formed a railing for the porch.

From the hut, the tangled thicket obscured the bay and, from the bay, an endless wall of trees and swamp ran down the coast.

Eddie stopped the engine and jumped up on the dock. Rico threw him a rope, untied Lucy, and pulled off the bag. Eddie grabbed her by the arm and pulled her up on the dock.

"Let go of me!" Lucy tried to pull away.

Eddie tightened his grip. "Shut up!"

Rico pointed the flashlight and moved ahead of the other two into the hut and lit a gas lantern.

Lucy struggled a little and came face to face with her captors and shivered. With jagged holes cut out for their eyes and mouths, the black stocking masks gave the men an aura of evil.

The dimly lit room contained a wooden picnic table with benches. A folding chair sat in the corner next to an army cot. Tacked to the rafters, a mosquito net hung over the bed. An old, black, wood-burning stove sat on the other side of the room.

"I've got to go to the bathroom."

The masked man holding her grunted and pushed her into a room and shut the door. "Hurry up."

Light from the other room slipped under the door and Lucy could make out a toilet, with a bucket of water sitting next to it. There were no pipes and no plumbing, and pouring the water from the bucket into the toilet would wash the waste down into the mangroves. The place smelled of human excrement, and the bugs flying about made Lucy twitch and swat at them in the dark.

The two men had spent the last few days at the shack, readying it for

Lucy. They had bolted a long pipe to the wall in the back room. Eddie handcuffed one of Lucy's hands to the pipe. The handcuff slid on the pipe, so she could walk from one end of the windowless room to the other.

"If you're quiet, we won't hurt you," Eddie growled. "If you make any noise or try to escape, we'll put the bag over you and tie you up again. Do you understand?"

"Yeah, I understand." She sat down on the bunk. Lucy shivered a little but she would not allow herself to cry.

Eddie and Rico walked to the door, and Rico turned back. "When you need to go to the bathroom again, bang on the wall." He slammed the door, and Lucy heard it lock.

On Saturday morning, Detective Verdona sat in the Medina's kitchen, a cup of coffee between his hands. Hugo poured himself his third cup, having had no sleep the night before. A yellow cab pulled up to the bridge. A policeman brought the cabdriver to the house. He had a letter for Hugo Medina.

"Who gave this to you?" Lou asked.

"Some guy in Miami. He gave me twenty bucks to deliver that envelope to this address."

"Could you identify the man?"

"Nah, he had sunglasses on and a hát pulled down on his head. I never got a good look at him. All I can tell you is that he spoke with a Spanish accent and that he flagged me down over on Flagler street near the river.

The note said:

We have her.

We want $500,000.

You will hear from us soon.

"The banks aren't open today. I won't be able to get that money until tomorrow, maybe longer. Now what?" Hugo asked the detectives.

"We'll keep searching for Lucy," Lou said, "and we'll check every lead.

The kidnappers will make another contact and another move—when they do, we'll get closer to Lucy."

"There must be something else we can do," Hugo's said. "Lucy is our only child. My wife is up stairs sick. What if they have harmed her?"

"Mr. Medina, I know this is hard, but the best thing you can do for Lucy right now is to remain calm," said Lou.

Hugo nodded and turned toward the glass doors at the back of the house. Staring out at the bay and the city beyond, Hugo went and stood in his yard at the water's edge. Behind the hotels along Biscayne Boulevard, the county court house rose up; its metallic, pyramid-shaped roof glistened in the morning sun. Lou Verdona walked up next to him. "Mr. Medina, are you sure you don't have some enemy out there? Possibly a business deal gone sour?"

"Like I told you before, Detective, I can't think of anyone who would have a reason to do this. Many people know I am a wealthy man. That's the only thing I can think of."

"Yeah, sure." Lou gazed at Hugo for a long moment, and then walked back toward the house. Hugo's thoughts tore at his insides as his stomach churned. He realized these detectives possessed savvy and intelligence and that they could help his daughter. He also knew that he could not prove Bernardo Gonzalez's involvement.

Hugo fought to control his trembling hands. *If Bernardo did have a hand in this, what could the police do in South Florida? What if they took Lucy to Colombia? The police might stumble and allow Gonzalez the time to make the evidence disappear. God, please keep Lucy safe.*

Hugo walked back to the house. Detective Verdona followed him to the patio, "Just remember, Mr. Medina, we can't help you if we don't have all the facts."

"I understand, Detective." Hugo walked inside.

Chapter 21

Carmen Medina's Idea

The next morning, the nine o'clock mass at St. Edward's was filled to capacity. The parishioners prayed for Lucy as her classmates and their parents lit candles in the rear of the church. After mass, groups gathered in the courtyard in front of the church. Mike stood with his family. He saw Francisco, Mrs. Medina's caretaker and driver, leaning against her dark blue Cadillac. Mike surveyed the crowd and found Mrs. Medina staring back at him. When he began walking toward her, Mrs. Medina turned back to the people around her, nodded and moved in Mike's direction.

"Buenos dias, Miguel."

"Good morning, Mrs. Medina."

She put her hand on Mike's shoulder. Mike saw the sadness in her eyes, but felt her strength and determination as well. "Miguel, as soon as you get home, please come to my house. Come alone. I need to talk with you about Lucy."

"Yes, Ma'am." Mike tuned and went back and joined his family.

Will motioned with his head. "What was that about?"

"Nothing."

Mike watched as Francisco opened the door and Mrs. Medina got into her car. She peered out the back window and gave Mike a slight wave.

After church, the Connellys went home and changed out of their Sunday clothes. The boys walked to Rusty's house, but Mike stayed for only a few minutes. He slipped away, walked past his house and around to the big gate, ducked under the wire fence, and ran through the coconut palms toward the house. As he approached the house, he saw Mrs. Medina in her straw hat, sitting in a high backed cane chair, gazing out at Stiltsville and the ocean beyond. Mike slowed down to a walk as Carmen turned her head toward him.

"Hello, Miguel."

"Hi, Mrs. Medina."

"Sit here, Miguel." She motioned to the other cane chair. On the low wooden table in front of them sat a frosty glass pitcher of lemonade and two glasses.

Mike read the headline screaming from the newspaper on the table—KIDNAPPING ON KEY BISCAYNE.

"Would you like some lemonade?"

"Yes, ma'am."

Mike's mind raced. *Why did she ask me to come?*

Mrs. Medina poured the lemonade. "Miguel, those men took Lucy away in a boat. The police think the boat sped across the bay toward Miami. They have not been able to find a strange boat or any witnesses. The police say the kidnappers may have gone north up the coast or even up the river, where there are hundreds of buildings to hide in. They are searching there, in the Bahamas, and down south in the Keys. I don't think they have any clues and I believe that the longer Lucy is held captive the harder it will be to find her."

Mrs. Medina sat up in her chair, and bent closer to Mike. She spoke in a steady tone. "Your friends might know how to find Lucy. They might know where the boat went that night."

Her words hit Mike like a jolt of electricity. *I knew it! She knows... how?* As Mike pushed his chair back and stood up his eyes widened, and he nodded. *That's a great idea.*

"Miguel, I have felt the dolphins for years and I know you have a special gift. Remember, the knowledge of the wonderful ability you possess has been with me for some time. Please don't worry; your secret will always be safe with me."

He silently walked away from her. He turned back. Carmen stood next to the table and gave him a slight nod. Mike started to run as fast as he could toward the cove. *She said she could feel the dolphins. What does that mean? Maybe like I was before I could talk to them. I'll tell Nyla later, but now I've got to find the dolphins. She's right, the dolphins can help find Lucy. I know they can.*

Far out at sea, Nyla's pod swam in formation. They joined with another pod, and the two dolphin families swam along the edge of the Gulf Stream, hunting for schools of mackerel or yellowtail, two of their favorite foods.

Come on, boys. Pull them together, Nyla said in mock seriousness.

Corran laughed. *We're working as fast as we can.*

Naarin, help your old dad and uncle, Nyla said.

I am, Mom.

The male dolphins swam faster, clicking and screeching in a circle around the fish. The school of fish began to bundle up.

Okay, Risa said, *girls first.*

Shanti, Loa, Nyla, and the other females charged into the ball of fish. They snapped up the mackerel with the ease of picking up lunch in a cafeteria line.

Nyla announced, *Boys, your turn, have at it.*

The male dolphins charged into the school one at a time. They liked to come together like this. Working in a bigger team made it much easier to hunt and eat.

Nyla felt a far-away, turbulent feeling coming from Mike's mind as the dolphins swam in a circle around the school. Naarin darted in and snapped up a fish.

Good catch, Naarin, his dad cheered him on. Naarin squeaked.

After we're done here, let's swim toward the bay. I want to go to the cove and the inlet and try to locate Mike, Nyla said.

Why?

Oh, I don't know. I just sense that something's going on.

Okay. We're almost done here.

With more dolphins controlling the ball of fish, they ate as much as they wanted. Compliments and thanks passed between the dolphins and the pods began to say goodbye and move away from each other.

In a few minutes, Nyla's pod began speed-swimming toward Key Biscayne and the bay. They burst out of the water simultaneously, skimmed the surface, and then slid back under. Naar, Corran, and Farin's low trajectory leaps made them the fastest and most powerful swimmers, but no one in the family had trouble keeping up. Even youngsters like Naarin and Shanti could fly. The technique of speed-swimming allowed the dolphins to almost double their speed without doubling their effort.

Late Sunday afternoon, the dolphins passed the big steel lighthouse. Naarin and Shanti still shuddered every time they went past it. The pod slowed down as they came into the bay. Now Nyla could feel Mike's mind.

I'm going ahead, I'll be in the cove. Nyla turned at the entrance and saw Mike pacing on the beach.

Hello, Mike. What's wrong? She slowed down and eased up close to the beach.

I'm so glad you're here. I wasn't sure you'd come today. I need your help.

Are you all right?

It's not me. It's my neighbor, Lucy. She lives in the big house over there. Mike pointed at the Medina house, just visible above the coconut palms. *Two men kidnapped her the night before last. They escaped across the bay in a boat. The police have no clues. Do you think you and your pod could help find her?*

I don't know, Mike. If she's on land, there's not much we can do.

She might still be on a boat, or she could be out on one of the islands. The men might be moving her from one boat to another. Some dolphins might have seen her.

Naar and the others swam up, *What's happened?*

I'll explain to you later. Mike, we'll start passing the word. How will we know her?

She is a tall girl, with long black hair and tan skin. She had on pink pajamas when they took her. The men wore black and had black masks over their heads.

Mike, come back here tomorrow, late in the day, at about your four o'clock.

As the pod swam out into the bay, Nyla explained the kidnapping. They decided to get the entire dolphin community involved in the search. Naar, Malak and Eshu sped off to the Bahamas. Corran, Loa and Shanti swam down south to the Keys. Nyla, Risa, Farin, and Naarin stayed in the bay. They would search the bay and up the river.

Chapter 22

The Colombian

At 9:00 AM Monday, Hugo walked through the doors of the First National Bank. Stepping off the elevator, he walked straight into the president's office. The receptionist recognized him. "Mr. Medina, any word?"

Hugo shook his head, "Nothing yet."

John Binker walked out of his office. "Hugo, I can't believe this. Come in." He ushered Hugo into his office and the two men sat down on a couch.

"John, I'm going to need five hundred thousand dollars quickly."

John nodded.

"I'll give you the ships as collateral."

"Don't worry about the money. You, your family, and Medina Shipping have been good customers. I'll get this done for you today, Hugo."

"Thanks, John." Hugo remained expressionless.

"Hugo, there will be some paperwork you'll need to sign this afternoon. Will you be in your office?"

"I don't know. Call me and I'll meet you in my office or yours, whichever is quickest."

"Of course."

Hugo got up, and the men shook hands. "John, thanks again."

Hugo walked through the door on the side of the huge dark blue warehouse. The white letters M-E-D-I-N-A stretched from one end of the front of the building to the other.

A receptionist behind a counter acknowledged him. "Mr. Medina, we're praying. Any news?"

"No, nothing yet."

"Sir, Mr. Bernardo Gonzalez telephoned. He said he would call back."

"Thank you." A cold chill ran up Hugo's spine.

A few minutes later, the intercom buzzed, "Mr. Gonzalez on line one."

Hugo picked up the phone. "Hello," he said.

"Hugo. It's Bernardo Gonzalez. I heard about Lucy from our consulate in Miami. Any word?"

"No, no word yet."

"Listen Hugo, I am sending you the five hundred thousand dollars. It is a personal loan from me. We can talk about you paying me back after Lucy is safe."

"No, Bernardo, I've already raised the—"

Bernardo cut him off. "Hugo, this is for the many years of doing business with your father and you. Our current little disagreement doesn't matter. Trust me, my man will be in Miami this afternoon. I have to go to a meeting. I'll be in touch."

The phone went dead.

That afternoon, Tony Galdo and Lou Verdona sat in Hugo's office as Hugo told them about the phone call. "So, this Bernardo Gonzalez is an old friend of your dad's?" said Lou.

"He has done a significant amount of business with my dad and Medina Shipping, and he is an acquaintance of mine as well," Hugo forced a slight smile.

"Some acquaintance," Tony said. "You think he is sending you the ransom money?"

"Yes, that's what he said."

A voice came over the intercom. "A gentleman is here to see you, Mr. Medina. He says he has a package for you from Mr. Gonzales."

"Please send him in."

A thin man walked in, immaculately dressed in a light tan suit and carrying a leather case. The man's surprised and nervous eyes darted around the room.

"Hello, I'm Hugo Medina," Hugo put out his hand. The man shook it.

"I'm Julio Esperanza," he said without any expression.

"This is Detective Galdo and Detective Verdona of the Miami Police Department." The man nodded at them but kept his hand at his side. Hugo motioned and they sat.

"Mr. Gonzalez instructed me to deliver this to you." Esperanza nervously glanced at the detectives, as he placed the leather case on Hugo's desk and opened it to reveal piles of hundred-dollar bills wrapped in red bands. Esperanza closed the case, took a piece of paper out of his coat pocket and put it in front of Hugo. "Please sign this."

The document startled Hugo with its simplicity as he read it out loud. "I, Hugo Medina, acknowledge receipt of $500,000 from Mr. Bernardo Gonzalez. Repayment terms to be discussed at a later date."

Hugo glanced up at the two policemen and they both nodded as Hugo signed the paper. Julio gave him a copy as the two detectives watched in silence.

"I will be staying at the Fountain Hotel on Miami Beach. Contact me there if anything happens." A slight, almost unnoticeable smile came across Julio Esperanza's face.

Hugo shook his hand, "Thank you. I'll let you know when we have some news."

Esperanza nodded to the policemen, turned, and walked out. The detectives walked out behind him. Lou whispered to Tony, "Let's get a tail on this guy." Tony nodded. Lou walked back into Hugo's office.

"What should I do with this?" Hugo asked, pointing to the case.

Lou reached out and took the case. "With your permission, I'll put this in the safe at headquarters. One of us, or a uniformed policeman, will be with you and your wife until we hear from the kidnappers. It should be soon."

Chapter 23
Wave Flying

That same morning, the dolphins in the waters of the Bahamas, the Keys, and South Florida began searching around every boat. They found nothing.

With Risa, Farin, and Naarin following along, Nyla swam to the cove late that day. She could feel Mike's troubled mind—Lucy kept popping into his head. Mike sat on a big piece of coral rock near the water.

Hello, Mike.

Nyla. Have you found anything?

No, not yet. Many dolphins are searching, and if Lucy is on a boat and gets out on deck, we might see her. If they keep her below, we won't know. We can't feel her mind like we can yours.

Farin swam over. *Remember, Mike, if anyone talks about Lucy on a boat, we might hear them. We dolphins can hear very well.*

I just hope she's okay. Some of the kids at school are saying that she could be dead.

Nyla said the only thing she could. *We'll keep watching and listening, Mike. Come back here tomorrow at the same time.*

Mike looked at his Timex: 4:30. Mike remembered the dolphins knew the time without the aid of a watch.

Out in the Atlantic, a pod of twenty spotted dolphins swam lazily, a few miles east of the Bahamas. The quiet open sea, with its abundance of fish, few boats, and no fishing nets gave these spotted rovers a sense of freedom that they loved.

Pike and Finn swam about a hundred yards behind the rest of their pod when a distant whistle from the west hit them. The pod screeched and clicked back. A young female named Zuri, from another spotted pod, came speed-swimming toward them, reaching Pike and Finn first.

Hey, Zuri. What's up? asked Pike.

Hi, Zuri, Finn said.

Hi, boys. Listen, a friend of Mike's named Lucy was kidnapped by men in black with black masks over their heads. Dolphins all over the area are searching for her.

Hey, slow down. When did this happen? asked Finn.

Three nights ago.

Where?

Over in Biscayne Bay. They took her from her house on Key Biscayne — put her in a boat and raced off into the bay late at night. But nobody knows where they went.

Pike and Finn thought it at the same time.

Where are the others? Zuri asked.

Up ahead a little, Finn said.

As Zuri began swimming toward the rest of the pod, Pike and Finn turned to the west. *Hey, where are you two going?* Zuri asked.

The two big males didn't answer her.

As they sped away, Pike asked, *Are you thinking what I'm thinking?*

Sure. After we ate those lobsters the other night, and we were floating around in the bay, that boat almost ran us over.

Yeah. No one goes that fast on a dark night in the bay. They'd risk running up on a sandbar.

The two dolphins rushed west. The calm conversation between their minds belied their excitement and their speed.

Pike, do you think we're onto something?

I don't know. Let's just get over there and check it out. If we think we might have a clue, we'll tell the others. No need to do that just yet. We don't know if the girl was on that boat.

The pair swam past the islands and into the waters between the Bahamas and Florida. With the wind gusting, the ocean grew rougher, and the waves swelled. Rain squalls whipped up the water. These ocean athletes loved rough seas and great ocean waves.

The dolphin community considered Pike and Finn to be two of the most powerful swimmers in this part of the world, and they took speed-swimming to a new level. With phosphorescent water and foam trailing behind, they blasted out of a wave just below the crest. Flinging themselves into the air, they speared the next wall of water with barely a splash. With two or three quick, powerful flaps of their tails, Pike and Finn shot out the other side and into the next wave. Only a few dolphins had mastered this fantastic swimming skill that the dolphins called "wave flying".

Pike and Finn, considered themselves to be truly flying. The troughs between the waves might be ten to fifteen feet below them, and with a little arc in their flight, they could span fantastic distances. The two laughed and cheered and prodded each other on. Like five-hundred pound flying fish, the sleek rockets got into a rhythm, skipping from wave to wave to wave.

The next morning Pike and Finn shot past the lighthouse and entered the quiet waters of Biscayne Bay. The two dolphins began their echolocation clicking as they swam across the bay.

Here's the place, said Pike.

Yep. The boat came from over there and then sped toward the southwest. You know there's nothing over there but mangrove swamp. The boat probably swung south toward the Keys.

You're right. We'll swim along the mangroves to the south, but I need to find some food first.

Good idea. I could eat a whale. They both laughed.

Red snapper loved to swim in and out of the mangrove roots. The dolphins knew they could click and find the snapper easily—sound waves confused the fish, and loud clicks sometimes stunned them, making them easy pickings for the dolphins.

After they ate, the two dolphins swam south along the mangroves. They broadcast a series of clicks as they swam. The sound waves bounced back into their heads, giving them a perfect picture of their surroundings. The two swam along for an hour.

Finn suddenly stopped. *Hey, Pike. I saw something back there.*

What?

I'm not sure. Circle back around with me. They swung back in a wide arc to face a section of the great mangrove swamp. They both clicked. The sound bounced back. The picture came to them, vivid and perfect.

What's that?

There's a big hole in the mangroves. It's a channel of some kind, Finn said.

With Finn slightly ahead of Pike, the two swam up and into the channel, following their echolocation sound waves.

This channel turns to the south and then back to the west, Finn said.

Where is it going?

I don't know. Follow me.

Pike and Finn cautiously floated in the water. The shadows of the swamp darkened as the day ended. They both rolled to one side and saw the black hut up ahead, with a speedboat tied to a rickety dock. Men dressed in black with black masks walked out of the hut and down to the dock. They pulled off the masks and talked for a moment.

Pike and Finn sank below the surface without a ripple, their thoughts exploding.

This must be them, Pike said.

What about the girl?

She's got to be in the hut.

She could be dead.

Nah, if they had killed her, they wouldn't be wearing the masks. Yeah, you're right.

Let's move out of here. It's too tight and shallow. I don't like it.

You go contact the others. I'll stay here and watch, Finn suggested.

Okay. But be careful. Stay at the mouth of this inlet.

Pike shot out into the bay.

After some time, Pike found Naar, Nyla, Risa, Farin and Naarin coming from up the coast and moving into the bay.

Nyla, Finn and I think we found her, Pike reported with an air of pride.

Where?

Over to the south in the mangroves.

Did you see her? Naar asked.

No, but we found two men with black masks in a strange hut in the mangroves.

Well, that is surely suspicious, Nyla said. *It could be where they're hiding her. Naar, you and Naarin come with me. Risa, Farin, contact as many of the others as you can. Tell them to come to the bay.*

Right. We're off! said Risa. Rising half way out of the water in unison, she and Farin spun and shot away, skimming over the surface. Nyla watched them for a moment, satisfied that many dolphins would be contacted by the speed swimming pair. In a matter of hours, a large number of her extended family and friends would be on their way to Biscayne Bay.

Okay, Pike, let's go. The dolphins sped toward the coast and the darkness of the mangrove swamp. Finn swam around in front of the hidden channel as the others arrived.

Anything happen? asked Pike.

Yeah. One of the men got in the boat and headed up the coast toward Miami. I've been up there watching, but nothing else has happened.

Nyla poked her nose in the channel and clicked a little. *Come on, Finn. Show me. The rest of you, stay out here.*

Mom, can I go? Naarin asked.

No, stay out here with your dad and Pike.

Stay out here son, Naar added in a fatherly tone, *Help Pike and I keep watch. We don't want anyone trapping your mom and Finn up in that channel.*

Okay, Dad. Naarin circled out in the bay.

Finn and Nyla swam up the channel. They both rolled over with one eye out of the water. A light shone through the screen door and the two windows. A man sat near the door.

This has got to be the place, she said. *Why would they hide the entrance? Why else would they be here?*

The pair turned and slipped back out to the bay. When they got there, Nyla gave her orders. *I'm going over to the Key and tell Mike. Naarin, you come with me.*

Okay, Mom.

The rest of you, stay here and keep watch.

Nyla and Naarin swam toward Key Biscayne.

Chapter 24

Darkness on the Bay

Mike lay tossing in his bed, thinking about Lucy, when Nyla's thoughts hit him.

Mike, are you awake? We have news.

Where are you?

Out at your dock.

Mike climbed down out of the bunk, causing Will to stir. Rocky trailed along as Mike slipped out the back door and ran to the ramp.

What did you find out?

Two of our friends may have found Lucy. We haven't actually seen her, but they have found men with black masks hiding in the mangrove swamp far south in the bay. You must tell someone.

How can I tell someone I found out about Lucy from dolphins?

Nyla's mind paused. *What do you want to do?*

Mike ran toward the house. *Wait for me. I'll be right back.*

Quietly, Mike picked up his shorts, shirt, and sneakers. He ran back to the boat ramp, put on his clothes, and then pushed the little boat toward the water. The boat made a scraping sound as it slid on the concrete ramp and Mike hoped no one had heard the noise. Rocky sat and watched.

Mike kept the engine off, and rowed down the inlet. Nyla swam next to him. *Mike, what are you doing?*

I'm going to try and make sure Lucy's there. Then I'll get help.

No. One of the men is there in the hut. It's too dangerous.

It's dark and spooky over there, said Naarin.

I have to go and see for myself and then go tell my dad. Don't worry.

When Mike got to the end of the inlet, he cranked the engine. With Nyla and Naarin swimming next to it, the little boat sped off across the bay.

Show me where I'm going. Don't let me hit anything.

Just follow us, said Nyla.

Nyla and Naarin sped ahead of Mike's boat. Even at full throttle, the little boat could never keep up with these speed-swimming dolphins.

Hey, guys, slow down. I'm losing you.

With no moon and only the lights of Miami reflecting off the bay, the mangroves appeared as a shapeless barrier of entwined trees and roots.

We're almost there. Let's slow down, Nyla said.

Cutting off the engine, Mike started to row with one oar. Soon he sat a boat length from the tangled web of mangroves with only blackness behind it.

Finn called to them, *Mike, right over here.*

Finn showed Mike the entrance to the channel. Mike struggled with the big branch but shoved it out of the way. He inched into the dark hole using his oar against the branches and roots. The boat scraped against the mangrove roots and branches as Mike pushed along in the narrow channel. He made very little noise and he was sure no one could hear him.

The twisted, bent mangrove branches hung down and enveloped Mike, hiding the sky and the bay. Mike could feel the darkness; he could hear the scurrying, and scratching in the trees as the mosquitoes and other flying things buzzed around him. The dolphins nudged Mike's boat along. He whispered, "Thanks," and reached over and stroked a dolphin's back. *Pff, pff, pff.* Mike nodded. His boat turned back west in the channel. Up ahead, a dim light glowed through a door and two windows. Mike moved closer.

Mike, this is not good. Let's just go get help, Naar said.

I want to get closer. Maybe I can see Lucy.

Mike slipped his boat up to the dock and held on to the post. Standing up, he could peer through the screen door and into the hut, but no one seemed to be around.

I've got to get the police, Mike said. *I'll tell them I just stumbled on this place.*

Mike, watch out! Naar's thought blasted out, but just a little too late.

Mike heard one footstep on the dock, as a man stepped out of the dark. With one powerful hand, he grabbed the back of Mike's shirt, and pulled him out of the boat and onto the dock. Mike struggled, but the man had him in a bear hug. He threw Mike up on the porch, holding him by the back of his pants and dragging him through the screen door. Mike winced, as the man grabbed his hair and twisted. His eyes and mouth popped out from behind a black mask.

"What are you doing here, boy?" The man growled, as Mike saw the silver pistol tucked in his belt.

"Nothing, I'm lost."

"Are you alone?" The man pulled on Mike's hair, harder. Mike almost cried out.

"Yeah, yeah, I'm alone. Hey come on that hurts! I'm alone." Mike tried to twist away, but the man held him tight.

The man in black dragged Mike over to the solid door, unlocked it, and pushed him inside. As Mike tumbled on the floor, Lucy, still chained to the pipe, stood in the corner wide eyed. The man pulled out another set of cuffs and hooked Mike to the pipe. Squeezing his cheeks together, he pulled Mike's face right up to his black mask. Mike could smell his stale breath. "Boy if you make a noise or try anything, I'll kill you and feed you to the crabs."

The man walked out and locked the door.

Dolphin voices came to Mike. *Mike. Mike. Are you okay?*

Mike, what's happening?

Are you hurt?

I'm okay. Lucy is here. She's okay. We're chained to a pipe. Get help.

Okay.

Even in the dark Mike could see Lucy's expression. "I don't believe it, Mike, what are you doing here?" she whispered. "How did you…"

"Hi, Lucy, you okay?"

"What are you doing here?"

"I found you by accident."

"What do you mean?"

"I was riding around searching for you, and I found this place."

"In the dark, in the middle of the night?"

"Don't worry about it, Lucy. Let's figure out how to get out of here."

"I've been trying to pull this pipe off the wall. Now that you're here, maybe together we can get it loose."

The two quietly pulled on one end of the pipe, but it never budged. After a while they gave up and sat next to each other on the cot, exhausted.

"I don't know how you got here, but thanks," Lucy whispered. "I've been pretty scared."

"I'm scared too, but don't worry, we're going to get out of here."

Mike sat on the floor and Lucy sat on the cot leaning against the wall. A boat motor rumbled outside.

"A boat," Lucy said.

Sitting straight up, Mike held up a hand. "Shhh." He listened as footsteps came into the hut.

"What's going on, where did that boat come from?" said another man's voice.

"Some kid came in here. I got him cuffed with the girl."

The door swung open. "Who are you, kid?"

"My name's Mike."

"Yeah, Mike who?

Mike paused for a moment, "Connelly, Mike Connelly."

"Where do you live?"

"Miami."

"Anybody know you're out here?"

"No."

"You know her?" He pointed at Lucy.

"Nope."

The two men walked out, locking the door. Eddie motioned to Rico as they stood out on the porch. He spoke softly. "Connelly—I know that name from somewhere. The kid has to know her."

Rico nodded in agreement. "You go tell the boss. Get back here before daylight with a plan."

Eddie got in the boat. "How do you think that kid found this place?"

Rico shrugged. "Luck?"

Eddie cranked the motor. "Yeah, bad luck."

The dolphins circled in the bay.

We must get someone to follow us here, Malak said.

Who? said Naar. *We could swim and jump around a Coast Guard or police boat, but they would never understand.*

How about the old woman? Corran asked.

She doesn't have a boat, Malak said, *and I don't think she would make the connection, go to the marina, and get out here.* All agreed.

We must go to the dome for help, Nyla said in a slow thoughtful manner.

Malak was the first to speak. *Do you think they will come?*

They took Mike down to the ship. He must be important to them, and I think it is the only thing we can do, said Nyla.

I hear an engine, Naar said. *It sounds like the speed boat is coming out of the mangroves.*

Farrin, Corran, Eshu, follow the boat, Nyla said. *Naar, you and the others keep watching, and go up the channel and speak with Mike from time to time.*

Make sure he knows he's not alone and let him know what's going on. Pike, Finn, will you come with me?

Sure, Nyla, they both said.

The three dolphins shot away to the east. Nyla picked these two powerful swimmers, knowing that they would pace her. She made herself keep up with them, as they headed out to sea. Nyla sensed Mike and Lucy did not have much time.

Farin and the others swam behind the boat as it approached the opening in the mangroves.

What happened? asked Naar.

He went up the river, got out, and in a little while came back to the boat and then came straight back here, Farin said.

Chapter 25
Two Fishermen

The smell of sizzling bacon drifted out of the kitchen as Alice shouted her wake-up call. "Let's go boys!"

Jim poured himself some coffee. Will and Bob walked into the kitchen. "Good morning, boys," Alice said.

"Hi, Mom." The boys sat down.

Alice gave them both glasses of orange juice and turned back to the eggs on the stove. "Where's Mike?"

"I think he's still sleeping," Will said, as he reached for a piece of toast.

"That's not like Mike." Alice put the plates of eggs on the table and walked down the hallway, checking the bedroom, and then the bathroom—no Mike. She walked back toward the kitchen and noticed that he wasn't at his usual perch out on the dock. "I can't find Mike."

Jim put the paper down and walked out into the backyard and noticed the empty boat ramp. He shouted down the inlet, "Mike! Mike!" Jim came back into the house. "The boat's gone." Puzzled, Alice went to the phone. Jim went back and threw on his clothes.

As Jim came out of his room, Alice hung up the phone. "He's not at the Butler's or the Medina's."

Within fifteen minutes, the entire police force of the Key had converged on the house. Jim and Alice stood in the living room, talking to a police sergeant.

Tony Galdo and Lou Verdona walked in the open front door.

"Thanks for getting here so quickly," Alice said. She faced the detectives and said, in an uneven voice, "We think he might be out in the boat searching for Lucy."

Lou turned to one of the policeman. "Radio the Marine Patrol. Give them a description of the boy and the boat." He turned back to Jim and Alice. "Any idea when he might have taken off?"

Jim said, "No. But if I had to guess I'd say early this morning."

Lou turned back to another man in uniform. "Go tell them to make sure to search up the river and south into the bay." The policeman turned and walked toward the door.

"Mr. Connelly," Detective Galdo said, "have you had any business dealings with Hugo Medina?"

"No, I own the drugstore on the corner."

Alice's eyes darted at Jim and back at the detectives. "You don't think Mike has been kidnapped, do you?"

"Let's hope not, Mrs. Connelly," Tony said. "I'd like you folks to stay home. Keep your boys home from school today and wait to hear from us. There'll be a uniformed policeman out front until we find Mike."

"Don't worry, folks," Lou said forcing an awkward smile, "he's probably out riding around in the bay."

Tony and Lou walked out in the front yard, talked to a few of the uniformed policemen, and then drove away.

"Alice, stay here with the boys. I'm going down to the marina."

"That's not what the police said to do."

"I don't care. Mike's not their son. I'm going to get some of the fishing captains to help." Jim ran out the door and jumped in the car.

Pike, Finn, and Nyla swam back toward Miami at a frantic pace. Nyla worked hard to keep up with Pike and Finn. The three crossed the Gulf Stream, and now when Nyla came up out of the water, the big steel lighthouse began to rise up in the distance, outlined against the afternoon sun. With the end of her marathon journey near, she pushed herself even harder as every muscle in her body strained.

The three dolphins came across the shallows. The barrage of sound waves grew louder as they swam. Now more than fifty dolphins circled around in the bay. Nyla swam to the opening in the mangroves.

What's happened? she asked.

Nothing, Naar said. *We've been communicating with Mike. He's chained to a wall, but he and Lucy are okay.*

Help is on the way, Nyla said.

Who's coming?

Krondal is sending help.

The dolphins continued to circle. *I hear a boat,* a dolphin said.

It sounds like an island fishing boat.

Yes, I think it is.

It's coming this way.

As the last light left the sky the dolphins watched the old fishing boat putter across the bay. The large, open boat, painted almost entirely red with yellow and blue stripes, had an engine in the middle and a long, black exhaust pipe sticking straight up. In the boat stood two, lean, dark men who appeared to be Bahamian fishermen.

In the deepening darkness the Bahamians eased their boat up to the mouth of the narrow cut into the mangroves. Discovering that their boat could not fit up the channel, the two men turned off the engine and pushed the boat back away from the opening. They tied up to the mangroves.

The fishermen said nothing as they walked to the edge of the boat, stepped off the side, and silently floated above the water and through the thicket of tangled trees. They glided straight toward the hut through the swamp.

Corran and Eshu swam up the channel. They surfaced right below the hut.

Mike, can you hear me? Corran said.

Yes.

Mike, some men are coming to get you out of there.

Where are they?

They'll be there any minute.

Mike had been sitting on the floor next to the cot, but now he jumped up and stood bolt upright, staring at the door. Lucy sat up on the cot.

"What's wrong, Mike?"

"Nothing, just be ready."

"Ready for what?"

"We're getting out of here, just be quiet."

Puzzled, Lucy stood up. "What are you talking about?"

"Shhhh."

Eshu rolled over and watched two men with black masks slip out the screen door and move around to the back of the hut. The fishermen touched down on the dock.

Rico stepped out from behind the hut to the left. He had a flashlight in one hand, and a pistol in the other. He pointed the light at the men. "Stop!" he shouted.

The fishermen kept walking. Rico pulled the trigger again and again. Eddie stepped out from the right and began firing. The bullets struck something just in front of the men and then disappeared with a little spark.

Lucy jumped. "What's happening?!"

"Stay calm, Lucy, I think it's over."

"Who's shooting?"

"I'm not sure, it's going to be okay."

A mental blast from one of the fishermen hit Rico. Grabbing his head and screaming, he dropped his gun and flashlight and fell to his knees, and then flopped forward. Eddie started backing up. The other island man stared at him. Eddie dropped his gun, groaned and fell on his back. The fishermen calmly walked around the motionless lumps as their flashlights lay on the porch beaming into the darkness and the twisted mangrove branches.

Mike and Lucy stood wide-eyed as footsteps came toward them and the door opened. As light spilled into the room silhouetting two men, Lucy tugged at the steel bar.

"It's okay, Lucy."

"Are you children hurt?" One of the men spoke out.

"No," Lucy said. "Help us. Get us out of here."

The man smiled broadly. "Not to worry, we're here to set you free, young miss."

With that, he grabbed the cuff around Lucy's wrist. It fell off. The other man freed Mike.

"Thanks," Mike said rubbing his chafed wrist.

"Thank you," Lucy managed a smile.

"No problem."

The four of them hurried out into the light of the front room. Mike noticed that the two fishermen both had lumps on the side of their hands next to the pinkie finger, lumps identical to the ones he had noticed on Mr. Crain and Darius.

Lucy touched one of the men on the arm as his eyes sparkled. "Who are you?"

"We are from the islands. We found you and now you're free. Come, children, Let us get out of this evil place."

I know who they are. I wish I could tell you, Mike thought.

The two men gave Mike and Lucy the flashlights, and they ran outside and down to the dock. Eddie and Rico lay motionless on the porch. The fishermen helped Lucy and Mike into Mike's boat.

"Go quickly now. Head for Key Biscayne. When you get there, tell the police where this place is and tell them to get here in a big hurry."

"You bet I will, and thanks a lot."

One of the fishermen untied the boat and pushed it away from the dock. "Now go."

Mike got the little engine running. He pulled away from the dock and ran right into the mangroves on the other side of the channel. Lucy pushed the boat away from the twisted roots of the mangroves, and then the boat rocked as something bumped it from below. Mike watched as Lucy pointed the flashlight down at the water. She jumped a little as dorsal fins and the *Pfff* of dolphins breathing popped out of the dark water. She pointed the light at Mike then back at the water. "Do you see them?"

"I know, Lucy, stop shining that light in my face."

Are you and Lucy okay, Mike? asked Malak.

Yeah. I'm just having some trouble with the boat.

We'll guide you out, Naar said. Naar and Malak pressed themselves against both sides of the little boat and guided it down the narrow, dark channel.

Don't crank that engine up too high, Mike, Malak said, *you might chop up my tail.*

I won't. I can hardly see anything.

I know, but we can see just fine, Naar said.

The little boat popped out of the hole in the mangroves, and Mike smiled as he saw the dolphins gathered there.

Okay, now get out of here as fast as you can. Naar said.

Mike saw the lights of Key Biscayne and got the boat going as fast as it would go.

"Mike," Lucy yelled over the whine of the little engine, "what's with all these dolphins?"

Mike shrugged and shook his head, "I don't know."

He caught Lucy's doubtful expression, as she kept shining her flashlight across the dark water of the bay.

Who got them to come and free us? asked Mike.

We'll talk about that another day, said Nyla.

Those were two of the skwill, weren't they?

Yes they were.

They shot out into the middle of the bay. A boat barreled toward them as an intense beam of white light blinded Mike and Lucy. Red and blue lights began flashing on the large boat and a whooping horn sounded as a voice boomed out over a loudspeaker. "This is the police! Stop your boat!"

A few minutes later Mike and Lucy sat together on the police boat heading for the Key Biscayne Marina with Mike's little skiff towed behind.

Mike, make sure the police get to that cabin as soon as possible. We don't know how long those two men will stay unconscious, Loa said.

Right. Mike pointed, "Over there, that's where we came from." A policeman reached for the radio.

Lucy sat next to Mike. She whispered, "What's going on Mike? What's with all those dolphins?"

"I don't know, Lucy, let's talk about it later."

"There must have been a hundred of them. They helped us somehow, didn't they?"

"I told you I don't know, will you just forget it."

"How can I forget it?"

"We're free and we're going home. Think about that."

Mike turned away from her. *If I could only tell her, she would think it was so cool. She would think I was cool.*

The police boat pulled into the marina. Jim and Alice, and Hugo and Amparo waited together. Two policemen on the dock took the lines and helped the kids off the boat. Lucy ran and leaped into her mother's arms. Mike walked toward his mom and dad. Alice ran and hugged her son, crying.

A policeman approached the families. "Folks, Detectives Galdo and Verdona are on the way. They asked if you could wait for them for a few minutes."

The families sat on the big white boxes located along the dock as the detectives arrived. Tony Galdo spoke. "We have the kidnappers in custody. We got them at the hut in the mangroves fifteen minutes ago. Folks, we need to ask the kids a few questions, and then we can go home."

Lou started the questioning. "Lucy, do you think you could identify the men who grabbed you?"

"They always had masks on, but I think I would recognize their voices."

Detective Verdona smiled reassuringly. "Mike, how did you find Lucy?"

Mike had been thinking about this moment ever since he boarded the police boat out in the bay. He decided to tell as much of the truth as he could. "Last night I couldn't sleep, so I took the boat out in the bay and started looking for Lucy."

His dad frowned. Mike caught his dad's expression and continued. "I rode over by the mangrove swamp and saw an opening in the branches, so I went in."

Detective Galdo got close to Mike. "You found the opening in the dark?"

"Yes, sir."

"That was lucky, Mike," Tony Galdo tousled Mike's hair, "but then, you're a lucky guy."

Detective Galdo turned to Lucy and said, "You told the police on the boat that two fishermen set you free. Is that right?"

"Yes, sir."

"Did you recognize them?"

"No, sir."

"What did they say?"

"They just told us they had found us and that we should hurry and get out of there."

Mike would have loved to tell them about the dolphins, but he knew he couldn't. Galdo spoke up, "Okay, let's go get some sleep. We'll be around tomorrow to talk some more. We should be by around eleven."

As the families walked toward the cars, Hugo touched Mike's shoulder. "Thanks, Mike."

Mike nodded.

When they got in the car, Jim turned to his son, "Mike, why did you go out in the boat last night?"

"I couldn't sleep."

"What do you mean, you couldn't sleep."

Mike felt his dad's anger growing. "I was thinking about Lucy and I wanted to try to find her."

"We'll talk about this in the morning," Jim scowled. "But let me tell you one thing young man—don't you ever go out in that boat alone, ever again. You were lucky, you could have been killed."

Mike turned away from his dad's glower.

"Do you understand me?"

"Yes Sir," Mike mumbled.

Alice stared at her husband with a look that only a mother can give. She turned back to her boy sitting in the back seat. "We love you, Mike, and we're happy you're safe." Mike forced a smile.

In the dark waters, the dolphins gathered around Nyla, Pike, and Finn.

Mom, did you swim all the way to the islands and back?

Yes, son, I did.

Wow. You were really fast.

You should have seen your mom, Pike said. *She can wave fly with the best of them.*

Soon she'll be out-swimming you, Naar, Finn said.

I don't think so.

Mom, will you teach me how to jump the waves?

I think I'll let your dad and his friends do that. She motioned over at the big males congregating together.

With their minds chattering away, the dolphins swam in the bay until just before dawn. They had helped catch the kidnappers. They knew this would be another great legend that would be passed down for generations to come.

We should start moving out toward the open sea before it gets too light, Loa suggested. *People will begin to wonder why so many of us are in the bay.*

They agreed, and many groups started to swim south and east. The dolphins squeaked, screeched, and clicked as they moved, and as they located a snack, they shot to the bottom, plucking the little lobsters and prawns out of the grass.

Most of the group moved out to sea. A dozen big males swam ahead and soon circled a school of silvery mackerel. Nearly a hundred dolphins caught up and began working together for a big meal. The pods enjoyed the camaraderie of these gatherings, and the bait ball of fish would be remembered as one of the largest they had ever experienced.

Naar and Nyla, with their pod and a few others, moved back toward the big lighthouse and Key Biscayne. Nyla wanted to make sure Mike and Lucy were okay. The pod swam close together.

Nyla, did you talk to one of the Teachers when you went to the islands? Risa asked.

No, I spoke to Darius. He and another skwill changed their appearances and came to Miami.

It is unheard of for them to do something like this.

Krondal probably directed them to come. He and the others must have something in mind for Mike.

Chapter 26

A Brave and Lucky Guy

In the morning darkness, Carlos talked quietly in the phone booth on the street.

"Señor, no one showed up. I think something went wrong. We came back into the bay at about two this morning. There were four or five police boats on the south side of the bay.

"Okay, Señor Gonzalez. I'll call you at two, and don't worry; there won't be a trace."

In Colombia, Bernardo Gonzalez dialed another number. The conversation lasted a few moments.

A few people moved about in the early morning. The impeccably-dressed man stood out in the old Miami Beach neighborhood. Julio Esperanza climbed the wooden stairs to the third floor, checked the gun in his belt, and knocked on Carlos' door.

"Who is it?"

Julio whispered, "I have a message from Bernardo."

The door opened, the ever-present chain stretched across the opening. Julio barely smiled. The door closed, and then opened wide, and he stepped in.

Julio had just finished wiping down the apartment when he heard car doors slamming outside. Peeking out the window to the street below, he saw that four police cars had pulled up in front of the building. Julio stepped over the lifeless body and walked out of the apartment at a brisk pace. He slipped down the rear stairs and walked out into the alley. He heard the sound of footsteps running into the building behind him as he walked away and disappeared into the labyrinth of narrow streets weaving through the art deco apartment buildings.

The detectives arrived late to the Connelly house. Sitting on the dock, Mike watched the men and his mom walk out the back door. Tony Galdo waved at Mike. "Hey, Mike. How are you doing?"

"Fine."

Tony stood against one of the pilings on the dock; Lou sat at the table next to Mike and Alice. The two asked Mike a lot of questions and wrote furiously in their little notebooks. Lou asked, "So, Mike, did you recognize the two fishermen?"

"No."

"Did you see their boat or watch them leave?"

"No, Sir. We just took off."

The two detectives turned to Alice. Lou said, "We forgot to tell you, the two bums we picked up have confessed. An attorney will be in contact with you about a hearing or trial, but since we have a confession your son may not even need to appear in court."

"Thank you so much," Alice said.

The two men nodded. "You're a brave and lucky guy, Mike. But don't go roaming around on the bay at night. Okay?"

Mike and Alice walked through the house with Lou and Tony.

Mike watched the two detectives walk down the street toward Lucy's house. He thought. *What will Lucy say? She can't say anything different than I said. It's what happened—well it's sort of what happened.*

The detectives talked to Lucy for an hour.

"So, Lucy, is there anything else you want to add?" Tony asked.

"No—well, just one thing, the dolphins."

"Dolphins?" said Lou.

"Yes, there were dolphins in the inlet when we escaped and when we got out in the bay there must have been a hundred of them around the boat."

"That's strange." Lou said.

"Yeah, it was weird. They always seem to be hanging around Mike."

Lou and Tony walked out the front door with Hugo.

Tony Galdo continued, "As we said, Mr. Medina, we don't think these two acted alone. Whatever they had planned has come apart—just be careful."

The detectives did not mention the dead man in the apartment.

Hugo stood next to the police car. "I've got to get Mr. Gonzalez's money back to him."

"Yeah, we talked about that," Lou said. "We'll handle that for you. Give us Gonzalez's number, and we'll contact him to make the arrangements."

Hugo hesitated. "I think I'll call him myself. He did give me the money, and I think it's proper that I talk to him first."

"That's okay, Mr. Medina. Just let us know." Lou got in the car, and the detectives drove away. "This whole thing smells," Lou said.

"I agree, but at least the kids are safe."

A few days later Lou Verdona sat at a metal desk in a room full of desks at the Miami Police Station. Piles of paper covered his work area. Sipping a cup of coffee, Tony Galdo sat across from his partner. Lou opened the folder in front of him. He had written some notes on a piece of yellow paper. "I tell you, Tony, none of this makes any sense. First, the two guys we catch are from Colombia. The dead guy is from Colombia. Medina does a lot of business in Colombia. Bernardo Gonzalez is a Colombian government official. He sends the ransom money up here with some vague repayment terms. This case keeps banging around in my head. I couldn't sleep last night."

Tony sat up and drank a little more coffee.

"Next, the boy just decides to go riding around in the bay at night. By some miracle, he finds the opening in the mangroves that happens to lead to the hideout. You know, Tony, I went back down there the other night. I couldn't see a thing; I mean I couldn't see my hand in front of my face, and the kid didn't have a flashlight.

"Then the two fishermen show up. How did they find the place? They sneak up on the dock. A bunch of shots are fired, but nobody gets hit. The kidnappers get knocked out. When we find them, they're still out, and these two can't tell us what happened. By the way—neither of them had a mark on them."

Tony shrugged his shoulders.

"How about this?" Lou began to get a little agitated. "Both kids told us that the fishermen came into the room and unlocked the cuffs. We found the keys to the cuffs in Rico's pocket. So what did these guys do? Knock Rico out, fumble around for the keys, unlock the kids' cuffs, and then put the keys back in Rico's pocket — all in the dark? It doesn't make sense.

"And then there are the boats. Mike said that when he got there, he pulled up to the dock. Eddie shows up later. Now there are two boats in that narrow channel. Then the two island guys pulled in there. The kids said that a few minutes passed from the time they heard the shots to when they got in their boat and took off. Lucy said that when they got in their boat they could hardly turn around. Three boats could never fit in that space. So where was the island guys' boat?"

Tony just sat there.

"How about the two fishermen? They didn't hang around for a pat on the back, a thank-you—nothing. They just disappear. And one last thing, Lucy's comment about the dolphins—what was that about? I just don't get it. I'm going to keep digging into this."

"Listen, Lou," Tony leaned up on the desk, "you and I have been cops for a long time, and we both know there are a lot of loose ends in this case. But we've got two bad guys, with confessions, sitting in jail, and the kids are safe. Between us, we have a pile of cases to work; so let's put this one on the back burner and go catch some more bad guys."

Lou closed the file. "You're right. But I tell you, that Connelly boy is one lucky young man."

Chapter 27
The Pendant

Sipping a Coke, Mike sat at the dining room table.

"Mike," his mom called from the kitchen, "Lucy's grandma is down at Lucy's house. She called and said she's stopping by here in a little while to visit with us."

A little later, Carmen knocked on the front door.

"Hello, Alice."

"Please come in, Carmen. How are you?"

"Now that Lucy is safe, I'm fine. Where is Miguel?"

"Oh, he's out back."

"Do you mind if I walk out there and talk to him?"

"Of course not."

"Hello, Miguel," she said as she walked up.

"Hello, Mrs. Medina."

"How are you feeling?"

"Great."

"Are you waiting for your friends?" She stood next to Mike and looked down the inlet.

Mike nodded but didn't say anything. *I have to be careful. She and Lucy are getting close to knowing. I wish Lucy knew.*

"They might be in the cove. Come inside with me. I want to give you something."

The two walked inside and Carmen stood at the dining room table. She took a tiny, black, felt box out of her purse and showed it to Alice and Mike.

"This belonged to my husband. I want Miguel to have it." Carmen opened the box. A 1 ½ inch long gold dolphin, with a green emerald eye, sat on the white silk.

Alice gasped. "Oh, Carmen. We couldn't allow you to ..."

"Please, Alice, this has been in my family for a long time. I have always believed that dolphins bring good luck and I insist that Miguel have it." She turned to Mike. "When you get older, I hope you will wear this pendant. Let your mother decide when the time is right." She handed the box to Mike.

Mike's eyes widened. "Wow."

"Carmen, this is much too much," Alice said.

"Miguel got back my Lucy, this is nothing compared to that."

Alice nodded. "Thank you so much."

Mike did not stop staring at the gold dolphin. "Thank you, Mrs. Medina, thanks a lot."

"Alice, can Miguel walk me home?"

"Of course."

"Come on, Miguel. Maybe we have a little coconut ice cream around that big old house."

Mike and Mrs. Medina walked down the street. They came to the gate and walked through. Mike always ducked between the wires of the fence, but not this time. They walked along toward the house.

"Have you thanked them for me?"

"No, Ma'am, not yet."

"You know, Miguel, I wish I could thank the dolphins myself, but I can't. Make sure that they know how much this meant to me. Thank them for my Lucy's life."

"I will."

"Well go ahead then," she motioned toward the cove, and Mike took off running as Carmen walked back toward her house.

As he ran his mind reached out, *Hey, are you in the cove?*

We're here Mike, a mind said.

As Mike reached the top of the little sand hill, he saw the dolphins out in the cove. He ran down to the water's edge. *Nyla, Naar, is that you?*

Four dolphins turned and swam toward the beach as the rest of the pod trickled into the cove.

Hello, Mike. Naar said.

Hey, Mike, you okay? Naarin asked.

Corran added his greeting, *Hi.*

Are you and Lucy okay? Nyla asked.

Yeah. We're okay. Please thank the dolphins for me. And Lucy's grandmother wanted you to know how grateful she is.

Lucy's grandmother? asked Naar.

You know, the woman who lives in the house over there, at the end of the Key, Mike said.

Does she know about us? Nyla asked.

No, She has an idea that I can talk with you, but she isn't sure how and why. Have you ever tried to talk with her?

We can feel her mind, and we have tried to reach out to her, Nyla said, *and I sense that she has tried to communicate with us, but she has never been able to break through.*

But how did she know to ask you to thank us? If she knows, this will be a problem for us. How did she find out? Naar asked.

Like I said, she knows something but she isn't sure what she knows. I think she has seen us together in the cove or the inlet, but I have never told her anything.

Perhaps an ancestor of hers had the ability to speak to us but she never inherited the full power, Corran suggested.

Nyla came to Mike's defense. *You know, Naar, the Teachers are sure that other people in the world have the potential to speak to us but their minds have not developed enough to break through.*

She told me she felt your presence, said Mike. *She said she felt something but she never knew what it was about.*

Be careful Mike, Naar said, *never acknowledge your power. Remember if anyone finds out about this, it could be dangerous for us.*

I understand, Mike changed the subject. *Who went and got the fishermen?*

I did, with two spotteds, Pike and Finn, Nyla said.

I know them. Tell them 'thanks'.

Risa spoke up, *Oh, they'll be around here again. You can tell them yourself. You know, Mike, I think Pike, Finn, and Nyla broke the record for speed-swimming from the islands to the bay.*

Mike laughed out loud.

Don't forget, you promised to read to us, Naarin reminded him.

Okay. Next time, I'll bring Treasure Island. *It's the story of pirates and buried treasure, but I'll only read it to you if you tell me* your *stories.*

Which stories do you want to hear? Loa asked.

All of them: The stories of the Indians, the pirates, the treasures and the submarines—tell me about the submarines.

Okay, Mike, Malak said, *we'll start next week.*

I can't wait.

Neither can we, said Nyla.

You know, Mike, we love it when you read to us, Shanti began to recite.

I started early took my dog,
And visited the sea.
The mermaids in the basement,
Came out to look at me.

And frigates in the upper floor
Extended hempen hands.
Presuming me to be a mouse,
Aground upon the sands.

We love poetry, Nyla said.

The poetry is *wonderful*, Malak said, *but nothing like—*

Retribution, swift vengeance, eternal malice were in his whole aspect, and spite of all that mortal man could do, the solid white buttress of his forehead smote the ship's starboard bow, till men and timbers reeled. Some fell flat upon their faces, like dislodged trucks, the heads of the harpooneers aloft shook on their bull-like necks. Through the breach, they heard the waters pour, as mountain torrents down a flume.

That's fantastic, Mike said, *I wish I could do that.*

You can, Malak said. *Just concentrate. Anyway, you should see the whales when we tell them the tale of Ahab and* Moby Dick. *They jump almost completely out of the water. It's great fun.*

When can I meet them? When can I watch them jump?

Someday, far out at sea, said Naar.

Mike and the dolphins talked until the daylight began to fade.

We should be going soon, a dolphin said.

Will you be going to the Bahamas? asked Mike.

Yes, and to the dome, Nyla spun in the water and headed for open water. *Good bye, Mike, we'll see you soon.*

Mike nodded, wishing he could go with them, but knowing that he couldn't. The rest of the dolphins followed Nyla and swam out of the cove. Standing on the spit of land between the cove and the bay, Mike waved both of his outstretched arms above his head as the dolphins leaped and spun in the shimmering bay, their bodies outlined against the setting sun. His mind raced—what could the Seegans possibly want of him, what stories would the dolphins tell, and why did he possess the power to communicate with them? He strolled through the coconut palms toward home. *I know one thing,* Mike thought, *I've kept my promise. I sure would like to tell, but I can't. I gave my promise and I'm going to keep it no matter how hard it is.*

Nyla's pod, and many more of the special dolphins, floated on the surface as the great dome rose from the sandy bottom.

The Seegans emerged inside, and the dolphins swarmed around the dome. Seegans waved and dove in the water as the dolphins swam into the dome through the passages.

Nyla came over to Krondal who sat on the edge of the walkway, with his long gangly brown legs hanging in the water.

Mike is safe. Thank you for sending the skwill.

It is against our beliefs to directly interfere, but we determined that Mike will be important to us in the future.

What do you think will happen?

Our relief ship should be here in forty or so earth years and we do not think we will just be able to slip away. Mike will be important to us when it is time to reveal ourselves to earth, and then leave this lovely blue planet. I only hope humanity doesn't destroy itself before then.

Oh, I think the humans will be just fine.

I hope you're right, humans may be able to control their aggression, but I'm not sure they will ever stop abusing their environment.

I suppose we'll just have to give them a little help from time to time—without their knowing it, of course.

Yes, Krondal chuckled along with Nyla. *We will help them a little.*

And we will stay close to Mike, Nyla added.

Tell everyone I said thank you for finding Mike and keeping him safe. By the way, that artist in Nassau is a skwill from the under Seegans. We are watching him. Tell Mike I said thank you for mentioning it. We did not know he was stationed there.

I will.

You know, Nyla, before we leave here we intend to reveal to this world how you and your kind have served humanity.

That will be a glorious day, Admiral, I hope I'm around to be a part of that.

Krondal dove into the pool, and as evening approached, the dolphins moved away, and the great dome retracted beneath the ocean floor.

Epilogue

Carmen sat among the palms near the water's edge and smiled. As Lucy walked up the driveway, she waved and began to run toward her grandmother. She plopped in the chair across from Carmen. "Hi Grandma. How are you?"

"Just fine, would you like something?"

"Yeah, how about a Coke?"

Carmen turned to the house. "Ophelia!" Ophelia stepped out on the porch, "Una Coca-Cola por favor!" Ophelia waved and disappeared back into the house.

"Have any of the kids been around today?" asked Lucy.

"No, no one has been by."

"What about Mike, has he been over at the cove lately?"

"I haven't seen him for a week or so, but then, I wouldn't know if he just walked over there without stopping by the house."

"You know, Grandma, lots of times when Mike is at his dock, over at the cove, or just near the water there are dolphins hanging around."

"Really, I didn't realize that," Carmen looked at her granddaughter with a blank stare.

"Sure, I think Mike has some kind of strange connection with the dolphins."

"What do you mean, connection?" Carmen maintained her expressionless gaze.

"I don't know, but it happens a lot. When we escaped from the mangroves that night, there were dolphins all around us. I think the dolphins had something to do with us getting out of there."

Carmen nodded.

"What do you think, Grandma?"

"Well, I believe there are people in this world who have a special feeling for animals. Maybe Mike is one of them."

"Mike with these dolphins is way more than just a feeling." Lucy's emphatic tone stabbed at Carmen.

"I don't know, my dear—Mike is the only one who can answer your questions."

"Yeah, I know, but I don't think he'll tell me anything."

The two talked for a while. Lucy finished her Coke, kissed her grandmother on the cheek, and walked off through the palms.

She found Mike, leaning against a rock, on the beach at the cove. A book sat in his lap.

"Hi, Mike!"

Startled, Mike sat up and watched Lucy walk over the sand dune and down toward him. He smiled a big grin. "Hi, Lucy, what's up?"

"Oh nothing," she sat in the sand and curled her feet up under her. "I was just over talking to my Grandma. What are you doing?"

"Just reading a little."

"Any dolphins out there today?"

Mike didn't move or turn his head toward Lucy. "Nope."

"That's funny—they're always showing up when you're near the water."

Mike turned toward Lucy, who sat close to him with a smirk on her face. "That's not true, Lucy, there's lots of times when the dolphins aren't around."

Lucy peered at Mike. "The dolphins are always near you. The whole Key is talking about it. Mr. Higgins says the dolphins are always coming up the inlet, and they never stop around his dock but go straight to yours. They never swim by my dock either. Why would that be?"

Mike shrugged and shook his head. "I don't know."

Lucy leaned over. "Mike, when those island men rescued us, you knew something was going to happen before it happened. Why did we have those dolphins around us when we got out of there? Did the dolphins tell you those men were coming?"

"That's crazy."

"Yeah, I know it's crazy, but I also know that when you caught that sailfish, dolphins had been swimming near the yacht and you knew that fish was going to hit. The dolphins told you to get ready, didn't they? And then there was that time at the beach club. When those huge dolphins popped up it scared me a little, but you weren't even nervous. You knew what they were up to."

"Listen to me, Lucy, there's nothing I can say. There's nothing I can tell you that would make any sense."

"You've got plenty to tell me, you just won't," Lucy got up and started walking up the beach.

Don't go, please don't go, Mike thought. *I want to tell you, I can't, I just can't. I made a promise.*

"Hey, Lucy," Mike ran up to her, "I know one thing."

"Yeah, what's that?"

"I would sure like some coconut ice cream right now."

Lucy smiled. "Okay, let's go get some."

Lucy and Mike walked up the sand dune and toward the big house. Mike cut his eyes and glanced back as a pair of dorsal fins cut through the water at the entrance to the cove.

BOCA RATON PUBLIC LIBRARY, FLORIDA
3 3656 0468091 9